Tracy Sorensen is an academic, journalist and film-maker. She was born in Brisbane, grew up on the north coast of Western Australia and now lives in Bathurst. *The Lucky Galah* is her first novel.

THE
LUCKY
GALAH

TRACY
SORENSEN

PICADOR
Pan Macmillan Australia

First published 2018 in Picador by Pan Macmillan Australia Pty Ltd
1 Market Street, Sydney, New South Wales, Australia, 2000

Cataloguing-in-Publication entry is available from the National Library of Australia
http://catalogue.nla.gov.au

Typeset in 12.25/17 pt Adobe Garamond Pro by Post Pre-press Group, Brisbane
Printed by McPherson's Printing Group

MIX
Paper from
responsible sources
FSC® C001695

Australian Government | Australia Council for the Arts

This project has been assisted by the Australian Government through the
Australia Council, its arts funding and advisory body.

To the memory of my father
Brian Sorensen

'This is the fishiest place I've ever seen,' wrote English buccaneer William Dampier during an eight-day stay at Shark Bay, halfway up the Western Australian coast, in 1699. The blue waters of the bay were alive with sea creatures. The following – about a man in horn-rimmed glasses and long socks who falls off a cliff – is a fishy tale. And yet all of it is true, as true as anything can be.

ONE

The Port Badminton Book Exchange

HER SHOULDER IS bony, her sinews defined, making a good perch. Her straight black hair – it's out of a bottle – hangs like a gentle curtain against my feathers. I can turn my beak into this hair, nuzzle into the scalp, or gently nip an earlobe.

She walks more slowly than I'd like. I want us to hurry up, to get there, but I'm restrained by the pace of her wandering shuffle; by the way she'll stop entirely, looking down at a twenty-cent piece on the footpath. There it is, sitting like an island in a drying splash of chocolate milkshake. Will her old knees survive if she bends down to get it? Yes. I lean back like a surfer or waterskier as she lowers herself to the ground.

We're on our way to the Port Badminton Book Exchange that adjoins the True Blue takeaway shop. These twin enterprises, housed in a brick rectangle, occupy a large area of gravelly, grassless dirt between the Caltex service station and the Olympic swimming pool.

I ride like an Afghan cameleer upon his ship of the desert. My face, belly and armpits are pink: a perfect pencil-box mid pink. My wings, back and tail feathers are grey; my crest is white. Charles Darwin, on his trip to Australia in 1836, commented on the 'excessively beautiful' parrots he saw; I'm sure he was referring to none other than the pink and grey galah.

The town of Port Badminton sits like a sandy freckle on the top lip of the open mouth of Shark Bay, just below the nostril of the Sandhurst River. The town is regularly whipped by tropical cyclones and inundated by foaming brown flood-waters. A decaying mile-long jetty reaches out into the Indian Ocean over shifting tidal flats. On dry land, yellow beaches give way to acacia shrub and low buildings surrounded by patchy grass and easy-care gardens of geranium, bougain-villea and succulent pigface. A wooden seawall curves at the base of the main street. The water here is flat, becalmed by a spit of mangrove land lying still and brown in the distance. There are date palms, and benches for sitting and watching sea and sky. The main street, perpendicular to the seawall, is a wide, hot expanse of bitumen. There are few cars, few people, moving about in the silent air.

We pause near the doorway of the Book Exchange. From here, we're in line of sight of the round white dish antenna that sits on a red dune just out of town. It's like the giant Jesus overlooking Rio, watching and keeping safe. People think it's dead, but they're wrong about that. It's still very much alive, sending and receiving signals. As a galah, I'm genetically predisposed to receive its signals. They're often – not always – interesting. Particular frequencies can give me a headache.

Lizzie is finishing her cigarette. Nearby, sitting side by side in the dirt, are a black dog and a yellow lemon. Is the lemon with the black dog, or is their proximity a coincidence? The dog lowers its head to lick the lemon. The lemon rolls away. The dog follows it and licks again.

Lizzie blows her cigarette smoke out of one side of her mouth, considerately directing it away from my face. She is watching the dog and the lemon, thinking her own thoughts. Her cigarette is now the tiniest stub of damp twisted paper. Lizzie drops it to the ground and grinds it into the earth with her blue rubber thong, the heel of which has worn down to the thickness of two pieces of paper.

We step inside, watched by the shop assistant with her indulgent little smile. We pause, letting our eyes adjust from outside glare to the relative dimness of the old fluorescent light. The light gives off a faint buzz. It is partly darkened by the silhouettes of dead flies and other insects. There are handwritten signs stuck at intervals around the room: *Crime, Sci-Fi, Romance, Adventure* and *Misc*. High on the wall at the back, on little hooks, are pastel crocheted baby dresses wrapped in plastic. Customers can pay cash for the books – the starting price is fifty cents – but they are encouraged to make use of the credit system, in which the value of returned books counts towards a new selection.

Lizzie will take a book from the shelf and show it to me, flipping through the pages. I make my selections according to my mood or line of thought. Some books have soft, pliable covers, easy to shred. Others have hard covers, requiring strenuous effort of beak, claw, muscle. Such books can keep me going for days, or a week, but they're often more expensive. Sometimes Lizzie is given a job lot of hard-to-shift copies of *Reader's Digest*. I'm not so keen – they're too easy, a mindless snack – but they're free, so we lug them home in a plastic shopping bag.

A shabby cardboard box at the far end of the counter catches my eye. A new delivery! In my excitement I screech and fan out my wings.

'He's spotted the box!' says the assistant.

'*She*,' mumbles Lizzie.

'Oh, that's right – she,' says the assistant.

She'll never learn. I'm a female galah. See my translucent red irises, like a glass of red cordial held up to the light? Male galahs have black eyes, opaque, like shiny beads.

We go over to have a look at the box. Good-looking books, some hardback. The urge to start shredding makes the strong muscles in my cheeks twitch.

'You like this one, Lucky?' asks Lizzie.

Lizzie holds a small blue hardcover book in front of me. It is *The Lore of the Lyrebird* by Ambrose Pratt. She leafs slowly through the first few pages. Mr Pratt was the President of the Royal Zoological Society of Victoria and his book was published in 1933. Lizzie skips ahead to the shiny pages. Plate 3 is a photograph of a lyrebird in profile, in silhouette, its lacy tail feathers held in an arc over its body. Its beak is wide open in song. Lizzie gazes at this picture. Until now, she has been showing me the book for my delectation, but I can tell that she is starting to take an interest in it for herself. It is to do with the stillness,

the extra dimension of quietness that now encases Lizzie
and the lyrebird. I feel a stab of jealousy like an electric
current. I pointedly turn my whole body around so that
I am looking away from the book. This means that I am
now facing the shop assistant. She is a woman with a large
bosom and a short grey fringe across her forehead. When
she sees me looking at her, she starts to sing.

'Dance, cocky, dance!' she says.

I dance, coquettishly.

'Don't you like this one, Lucky?' mumbles Lizzie. I can
tell she is still gazing at the lyrebird. I continue to dance for
the shop assistant.

'That one's ten dollars,' says the shop assistant, raising
her voice to speak to Lizzie, as if she were deaf. 'That's an
old collectable one.'

It is clear the shop assistant believes this figure will put
Ambrose Pratt's monograph out of Lizzie's range.

'Righto,' whispers Lizzie.

I stop dancing and the shop assistant raises her eyebrows.
'You're going to get that one, are you? It's *ten dollars*.'

'Yes,' says Lizzie more clearly, although she doesn't look
up. 'I'll have it, thank you.'

'Are you going to give it to the galah?'

'No.'

Rage fills my heart. It makes me rigid through the crop,
gullet, shoulders, neck.

Not letting go of the lyrebird – she tucks the book
under her left arm – Lizzie picks up another book, a small
paperback.

'Do you like this one?' she asks, holding it up in front of my face. It is *The Lucky Country* by Donald Horne. I sit stonily, unable to say yes or no.

'That one's fifty cents,' says the shop assistant.

When we step out of the Book Exchange, the dog has vanished but the lemon remains. It sits on the gravel, rocking almost imperceptibly.

Our books swing and bump in the worn plastic shopping bag as Lizzie lights a new cigarette.

DISH: Stand by.
GALAH: Roger.
DISH: Tropical Cyclone Steve latitude 25 longitude 113, wind gusts up to 140 kilometres per hour, central pressure 980 hectopascals. Headed this way. Over.
GALAH: Roger that.

Lizzie hears my double chirrup sign-off and thinks I'm talking to her.

'Home soon,' she says.

We move off in the direction of the boat harbour, where the prawning boats hold their nets up against the blue sky. Lizzie scans the ground. Sometimes she looks up, searching out birds. She rarely looks about at human-eye level. But I do. I like to see what people are doing, what they might be putting into their cars, what they might be chatting about as they stand with one arm on the open door.

I'm thinking about Luck. Luck rides on the wheel of fortune, round and round. The man on the top – Evan Johnson, for example – can find himself falling to the bottom. And the one on the bottom – me, for example – can suddenly be cast to the top, long after she'd given up hope. She might open her eyes, and look about, and realise she is now out of her cage. She might cautiously spread a pink and grey wing, feeling the unused muscles cramp and stretch in unusual ways.

That's how it was between Evan Johnson and me. On the day his fortunes fell, mine rose.

We pass into the cool, deep shade under the balcony of the Port Badminton Hotel. This is the hotel where Crowbar – the federal Minister for Regional Development – got his nickname. As a young man he'd struck a man about the head and shoulders with a piece of metal cable and was fined for assault. As the story was told and retold, the metal cable became sturdier and larger, until it emerged as a crowbar. Now known as Crowie, you can sometimes see him on television, standing outside Parliament House in his akubra and crocodile-skin shoes.

We glance in through the door, where it is dark with the smell of beer and the Underworld.

Back out in the glare, our eyes adjust. I can hear a wild galah shouting from a branch of the old eucalypt outside the post office.

'You ask her,' shouts the male galah. Lizzie looks up, squints into the darker recesses of the tree. 'No, you ask!' replies the female. To Lizzie, this is just squawking.

As Lizzie and I pass under the tree, the female galah – young and naive – calls out to me, more quietly, as if Lizzie might be able to understand.

'Is it true the old lady's a hundred and twenty years old?'

'No,' I reply. 'She's much older.'

The galahs are silent in their surprise. I enjoy teasing them.

'Hello, pretties,' mumbles Lizzie in the general direction of the young galahs.

A few blocks further along, we turn into Clam Street, where fibro houses on stilts face an expanse of salty, muddy samphire flats stretching out to mangroves in the distance. If you're lucky, you might see a slender-billed thornbill here, gently calling *tsip tsip*.

We pass the Johnsons' house. There are other people there now, but I'll always think of it as the Johnsons'. Next door, there's a pale pink house with an oleander shrub out the front. Nobody has ever been seen coming or going from it, although it would appear to be inhabited. After that, it's the Kellys. Kevin and Marjorie Kelly's small weatherboard house, complete with crumbling chimney, is much older than the others and sits low on the ground, slightly sagging into it. A long time ago it was painted in a strong blue, but the paint has scuffed and peeled over time, revealing the wind-worn planks beneath. Collected objects decorate the front garden. Some of these – old pots, a wellington boot – are planted with well-watered geraniums. Next to the front gate and letterbox, there is a white-painted swan made out of an old car tyre. Each year, its long sinuous neck drops lower to the ground. The red geraniums planted into its back are rich and perky.

DISH: Dish to Lucky the Galah. Stand by.
GALAH: Standing by.
DISH: Incoming rueful thoughts Marjorie Kelly. Sewing room latitude 24.894362 longitude 113.658156 in a stationary position.
GALAH: Not now.
DISH: Now. I must dump.
GALAH: Roger.

MARJORIE KELLY: I think Kev is writing a letter. I saw him get the writing pad out. He didn't know I was looking. His own breathing is so loud and he's that deaf, he doesn't know who's right there behind him. Nobody writes letters these days. The girls just pick up the phone and ring me. I used to say, 'This must be costing a bomb,' but they'd just laugh at me. 'Don't worry, Mum, we can afford it.' I still like to be quick on the phone. Kev's sitting at the kitchen table with a biro in his hand. I saw him slide the writing pad under the newspaper as I went into the kitchen to boil the kettle. He pretended he was doing the crossword. When I left he would've slid it out again.

I love sitting here by myself in my sewing room with a cup of tea, like I used to do.

I spent all day yesterday cleaning out the junk. I brung it back to what it was in the glory days. I lifted the cover up off the old green Pinnock and there she was, was my old friend. I gave her a good oiling, gave her a run. It's lovely to hear her go again. She worked hard for twenty years making dresses for local ladies. Then they started going to

Geraldton and Perth to buy off the rack. A trip that used to take days, they do at the drop of a hat, now. They all have air-conditioned cars. That put me out of business. I even stopped making my own frocks and started wearing stretchy shorts and drip-dry shirts.

Once upon a time, I would've been horrified to wear stretchy shorts outside the house. That's how much things can change.

I miss my frocks.

This one, for instance. Smells a bit musty. This was my maternity frock. I had five girls, one after the other, so you can imagine I got a lot of use out of it. It was very comfortable, very hardy. You could still wear it now, if you were petite. But it's too covered up for today's woman. It's all gathered from a yoke, falling right down below the knee. Now they just wear a little t-shirt with their bare bellies sticking out. I saw Kev do a double take in the street. I said to Kev, 'That's the style these days, they all do it.' And then a couple of days later we saw it again, another young girl with her swollen tummy showing. I knew Kev wasn't coping with it. He went red in the face, angry. 'Out and proud,' I said to Kev, to tease him.

He said: 'You don't know what that means, Marj.'

'What?'

'Out and proud.'

Yes, I do. He likes to think I don't know about rude things. He thinks I'm pure of heart and mind.

Maybe he's writing his will.

I've been going through all the old bits of material. I've got

scraps from all of them, every dress I ever made. All the girls'
clothes. Not their panties though. I made cotton panties for
them until they begged for shop-bought ones so they could
be like their friends. Scraps from all the dresses I did for Linda
Johnson. She'd come here for a fitting. I'd measure bust, hips,
her small waist. She'd hold her long black hair to one side as
I measured the length from nape of neck to small of back. I'd
get down on my hands and knees, circling her legs, getting
the hem level. Then we'd sit out the back and have a cup of
tea. I used to mind her littlies. I did a lot of babysitting while
she scooted around town in my lovely dresses. Linda brought
the compliments back to me. I lapped them up.

This is a piece from the dress she wore to the Moon Ball.
It'll do nicely.

She turned on me in the end. After her husband fell off
the cliff at the Blowholes. I went over with a pressure cooker
full of soup, but she shouted at me to *Get out, Get out.*
I came in here and cried for days. I was probably also crying
about other things. I got it all into one big cry. It's the same
as if you've got the oven on, put everything in that needs
baking. Not like now, when people will have an oven on for
one little thing.

Kev was good. He said to the kids, 'Leave her alone,
Mum's having a cry.'

My sister said Linda was mad with grief, she'd be friendly
again later. She also said maybe Evan jumped off the cliff
on purpose, maybe he wasn't the father of their little girl,
maybe the father was that enterologist that went out on
Kev's boat and she said in her opinion, Linda Johnson was a

13

snobby hussy and she hadn't wanted to say anything earlier because we were such good friends.

I said nothing.

'It was always "Linda this, Linda that",' my sister said, in her mimicky voice. She can be a real B-I-T-C-H.

I never saw that pressure cooker again.

DISH: Over.
GALAH: Roger. Over and out.

When we get home, Lizzie lifts the thin plastic bag onto the table. Her worn thongs slap on the linoleum floor. The house is silent. Not even the refrigerator is humming. I'm out of line of sight of the Dish; I can take a rest from its endless data dumps.

I hop-flap from Lizzie's shoulder to my high T-shaped perch. Lizzie flicks the radio on. It starts chatting immediately, all about Steve.

'Cyclone coming, Lucky,' says Lizzie.

'I know,' I say, but it comes out as a half-baked croon.

She opens her eyes wide, dramatically. 'Cyclone! It's pretty windy, hold on tight!'

'Pretty windy, hold on tight!' I say in English. In English, my voice is a quavering thing. We repeat this back and forth, enjoying ourselves, until I grow impatient and excited, accidentally letting out an ear-splitting screech.

'Shoosh, Lucky,' says Lizzie.

'Shoosh, Lucky,' I agree.

I watch as Lizzie puts the kettle on. She sets out a mug

for herself and a dainty teacup for me. While the kettle is boiling, she removes the two books and loose coins and the five-dollar note from the plastic bag. She folds the bag and puts it away in a drawer. She puts her money in an old biscuit tin. I gaze out the window at the purple bougainvillea in the neighbour's yard. Without looking, I can tell that Lizzie is putting *Lyrebird* in the same drawer as the bag and closing the drawer firmly. It's the drawer that contains a couple of back issues of the *Australasian Bird Fancier*, phone and electricity bills, and correspondence from the government relating to the pension. It is the Important Drawer. It is a drawer that I can't get my beak into.

The Lucky Country lies on the table. Later, Lizzie will nail it securely to my perch so that I can shred it with my beak without the book falling to the floor before I have finished. Lizzie shovels three heaped spoons of Bushells tea-leaves into a red anodised aluminium teapot and pours the steaming water in. She folds a tea towel over it to keep it warm, and carefully turns the pot three times. Lizzie holds out her arm, inviting me down onto the old wooden table.

She pours just a tiny bit of tea into my teacup and fills it up with cold water from the tap.

'This teacup went all the way out to the island and back,' says Lizzie.

She says this nearly every time. It's the story about how her mother went out to the end of the One Mile Jetty in chains, carrying a teacup, and took a boat to the island, where she lived surrounded by sharks, listening to the water crash and the wind moan.

15

When she came back, she thought she'd lost the teacup, but it found her again.

'Skippety-hop to the grocery shop,' I say. 'To buy a box . . .'

Lizzie joins in: 'To buy a box of candy. One for you, one for me, and one for sister Mandy.'

Three times, she dips a teaspoon into the pink paper sugar packet. The white crystals fall like a waterfall into her mug. Then she stirs vigorously, and takes a sip.

'Ah,' she says. 'I needed that.'

She feeds me pieces of Milk Arrowroot biscuit. I don't mind nibbling from her fingers, but I prefer to hold a piece of biscuit in my claw and eat it like that. I wash it down with tea. Lizzie smiles as I dip my beak into my cup and then point it at the ceiling so the liquid can flow down my gullet. I feel it swirling into my crop, seeping down into my gizzard.

I beg for another bit of biscuit.

'One for sister Mandy?' I say, with all the sweetness I can muster.

But afternoon tea is over. As Lizzie washes the cups and saucers in the sink, I make a start on *The Lucky Country*.

The galah is an intelligent animal, despite its reputation as a clown and lightweight. A captive galah needs constant activity if it is not to decline into depression. Tearing up books, page by page, is a mental, physical and spiritual workout for me; as good as any gym, yoga class or university.

Lizzie naps on the couch as I work. The *Australasian Bird Fancier* has slipped from her hands. Her mouth is slightly open. She snores.

The Lucky Country is a slim volume, paperback; faster to get through than an old *Reader's Digest*. I tear it up quickly, not expecting much.

Afterwards, I begin to doze off myself. As my nictitating membranes slide upwards over my pupils, the words of *The Lucky Country* come back to me, suggesting pathways for dreams. *The wooden salad bowl. The bead curtain. Innocent happiness.*

When I open my eyes, I see the remains of my book on the floor. Strips and straggles of paper. Part of the cover still readable, but the L is missing: *ucky Country.* A dustpan and brush come into view, and Lizzie's knobbly hand. She sweeps everything up – parts of sentences, torn words – in neat little strokes. She carries the pan out through the back door and I hear the smack of the wheelie bin lid before she reappears again.

I can still copy, perfectly, the flushing of the Kelly toilet. This makes Lizzie laugh her raspy little laugh.

She walks across the room and gives me a nice long scratch. When she stops, I continue to hold my neck out, inviting more.

'What are we going to do with you, eh?' she croons. 'My beautiful girl.'

I don't answer. My receptive vocabulary is excellent, but my productive vocabulary remains frustratingly limited. My spoken English progressed from *Hello, cocky* and *Dance, cocky, dance* to *Skippety-hop* when I came to live with Lizzie. Later I learned *Stupid dickhead* and *Ba-a-ad cough!*

Stupid dickhead came from evenings watching the tele-vision news with Lizzie. If she caught sight of Crowbar in his crocodile-skin shoes and akubra talking to reporters on the steps of Parliament House, she'd say, 'Stupid dickhead,' and I began to say it too. We'd look at each other and laugh. I'd repeat myself, trying for a second, third or fourth laugh, but there were diminishing returns.

Lizzie says, 'Bad cough!' in the mornings before she has her first cup of tea and cigarette. She wakes, she coughs, she looks at me and she gasps, 'Bad cough!' I cough along with her; enjoyable raucous coughs. She looks at me and says, 'Don't make me laugh.'

She lets me gently preen her hair. She lets me stand on the edge of the table and delicately lick up the biscuit crumbs stuck to the front of her dress. She likes to look at my tongue, the hard bulb on the end of it made for crushing grass seeds. Sometimes I lean in to her face and preen her eyelashes, one by one. Lizzie doesn't flinch.

I'm still thinking about those words. *Wooden salad bowl. The practical Australian.* It's as if they're rising up from the depths of the wheelie bin, slipping out through the crack under the lid, floating back to me on my perch.

I have worked from the beginning to the end of *The Lucky Country*, but I am still puzzled by its central idea. For me, *country* is everything that is here. It's the red earth meeting the dazzling blue of the Indian Ocean; the curling wattle pod at the end of a spindly grey twig; ribbons of seaweed in great rolls on the beach; the dark holes in old eucalypts where parrots are born. Country is alert and generous, but

18

still. It has been here for a long time. It throws up tiny green shoots after rain, but it's too old, now, to feel either lucky or unlucky. It just continues.

People and animals, on the other hand, are mostly young, or feel young. They still want things. I may have lived for decades but I still feel young; I still feel lucky. My life today – with its tea and biscuits, its frequent tours of the town – is bristling with enjoyments and advantages. It stands in direct contrast to my life Before, which was spent in a small cage in which I could not fully stretch my wings.

The trajectory of my life – from misfortune to fortune – is precisely the opposite of Evan Johnson's. His life began in fortune only to fall, fall into the maw of misfortune. This fall is fascinating, mesmerising. I study it in my mind's eye. I see a falling man, a rising bird.

Falling man, rising bird.

I am agitated, leaning this way and that on my perch, overwhelmed by the new story that is swelling in my throat. This happens sometimes, after I shred a book and become excited – desperate – to join in with the storytelling. I begin to screech, helplessly, telling, telling, telling.

My stories are made of found objects: shreds of text, parts or wholes of spoken phrases ('Did ya get drunk?'), data dumps from the Dish that come thick and fast as we enter its line of sight and stop abruptly if we turn a corner or retreat indoors; the popping of wattle pods showering story-seeds; the conversations of wild galahs flying overhead or gossiping on Lizzie's back fence; the secret messages sent by pet galahs, prisoners in their cages, garbled through

19

unreliable intermediaries. My stories are outsider art, self-taught, mostly stolen, highly embellished. They –

Lizzie groans.

'Shoosh, Lucky,' she says. She is rolling up her *Australasian Bird Fancier*, threatening to whack me with it. I'd better stop.

Anyway, this is the story so far, translated from screech to English:

TWO

The Practical Australian

IT IS 1964. Evan Johnson is young and alive from head to toe. His wispy blond hair is already thinning on top. He's at the wheel of his brand-new mid-blue EH Holden station wagon, a plume of pink dust fanning out from the back like a small willy-willy. As far as the eye can see in any direction there is low sage-coloured scrub dotted over red earth. Overhead, a cloudless blue sky.

Evan Johnson has just been given an extraordinary technical assignment and the promise of excellent pay. On the strength of this, he has bought the car and packed it with all the things most important and useful to him: wife, daughter, slide rule. He has filled the tank with petrol, checked the oil and water, settled into the driver's seat and started driving. He drives and drives and drives. He drives all the way from Melbourne, at the bottom of the continent, to his destination on the north-west coast of Australia. The gently waving stalk of his brand-new aerial catches voices speaking of Reds to the north and Blue Hills in the distance. They tell of the price of wool and a lottery in which numbered marbles

23

representing the birthdays of twenty-year-old men are to be drawn from a barrel and the winners sent to war.

In Melbourne, Evan Johnson had worked for an expanding national company that made televisions and radio transmitters and the electronic equipment found in ships and aeroplanes. Tomorrow morning he will start a new job with the federal Department of Supply to help establish a tracking station at Port Badminton. It takes days to drive there. At night he turns his gaze upwards to the jewelled night sky, studying the constellations.

There he is in his horn-rimmed glasses, shorts and long socks. One hand is pointing up at the heavens, the other is closed loosely around the slide rule. There is a sharpened pencil in his pocket.

For Evan, used to cold Melbourne winters, it is uncomfortably hot in this part of the country. He lifts each thigh in turn to unstick it from new blue vinyl. The vinyl clings to skin like a bandaid. The radio, struggling to keep hold of Jimmy Little's 'Royal Telephone', gives up and surrenders to static. No twiddling of the knob can help it now. Evan switches it off with a tiny click, felt in the fingers but not heard over the sound of the Holden juddering over corrugations in the road.

Evan is thinking about Time. As he drives, eyes on the road, always careful, his mind feels its way in the dark towards a thought about Time that is both simple and large, something very close, but eluding him all the same. After some minutes of struggle, he gives up. He lets go of the large idea of Time and relaxes into thoughts about smaller, more manageable pieces of it. In his mind's eye, he sees a space-craft appear on the horizon at precisely the right time. He traces its arc over him, mentally moving it across the hollow sphere of the sky, taking it down again below the opposite horizon. The golden hairs on his forearms vibrate with the shaking of the car. A trill of excitement burbles briefly in his upper abdomen. He emits the energy of it in the dry fragment of a whistle. He wets his lips and tries again, thinly whistling the melody: *Oh, what joy divine!*

When Evan Johnson lifts each thigh in turn to unstick it from the vinyl seat he does so without making any remark, because for him such a thing is not worthy of comment.

His wife, in a similar situation, would vocalise without hesitation: 'I'm sticking to the seat!'

But in this case Linda Johnson is not sticking to the seat, because she is wearing a white gaberdine dress with large red roses on it, cinched at the waist with a belt made of the same fabric. There's a long hidden zip down the back. All of this fabric, which goes down below the knee, ensures she does not stick to the vinyl seat of the Holden station wagon.

The car smells of processed cheese and celery and a warm pale green Tupperware container and a toddler's urine.

Lolling freely on the back seat is three-year-old Johanna. She is a little astronaut in a suit, carrying out her human functions in a moving capsule, patiently ministered to by the experts in the front seat. Her life is an endless car trip, like a rocket voyage to a faraway star, seemingly without beginning or end. Telegraph poles go past. Their wires swoop up and down, up and down and criss-cross.

She tastes a bit of cheese and Sao biscuit passed back from the pale green Tupperware container and lets the rest fall through her fingers. She notices sheep and says, 'Sheep!' Her parents say: 'Yes, Jo! Sheep!'

Her mother twists around to look at her lovingly, her face framed by her black hair, a long neck like a swan's. She says: 'Baa! Baa!' As she says this, her dark eyebrows lift twice, very expressively. She smiles with her red lips and long white teeth, and then turns around again.

Jo looks at her mother's long black hair. She tries to open the ashtray which for this entire journey has been sitting tantalisingly in front of her, attached to the back of her mother's seat, but it will not open. She nibbles the ear of her squeaky plastic lamb, tasting the plastic. She throws her lamb into the front of the car. It ricochets off the windscreen with a faint squeak and lands in Evan's lap. Linda cries: 'Jo! Don't be naughty!' Evan brakes and stops the car on the side of the road. He pauses and then turns around, coldly and deliberately, to face his daughter. His horn-rimmed glasses and light flyaway hair presaging baldness fill Jo's field of vision. She starts to whimper. Evan waggles his finger sternly. 'Jo, you mustn't throw things around the car. You're making Daddy very angry.' Jo finishes her current whimper, takes a breath, and howls. Linda and Evan glance at each other in solidarity, a quick look that excludes Jo; this does not escape her attention. She lies on her back, kicking her feet, punching the seat with her fists.

The beige ceiling of the car has side-to-side stitch lines. The clouds are wispy. The telegraph wires criss-cross, criss-cross.

26

Evan sees a small white object materialise in the distance on the left-hand side of the road. It is the next milepost. He is getting closer. His Expected Time of Arrival is 6 pm. Evan presses his black leather lace-up shoe just a tiny bit harder on the new accelerator pedal. The motor laps up the extra fuel and goes a little bit faster, but not, in Evan's opinion, dangerously fast.

Linda stares at the milepost too, at first wondering if her eyes are playing tricks. It is, indeed, a milepost. The numbers are close enough to read now. It is still a long way to Port Badminton but she is excited, impatient to begin her new life. She can smell the rich scent of her own body odour mixed with talcum powder. She feels an overwhelming urge to leave the car immediately. Excitement tends to play itself out in her bowels. Her left hand twitches slightly in the direction of the door handle.

'Honey,' says Linda to Evan in the little-girl voice she often uses with him, 'I think I do need to have another wee.'

A tiny stream of the molecules of irritation and impatience spurt into Evan's bloodstream. He takes his shoe off the accelerator pedal and steadily depresses the brake, bringing the car to a gentle stop beside nothing in particular. He is losing time, whole units of time.

Linda Johnson's pale long legs appear out of the side of the car like the front antennae of an albino lobster. It is 1964, and she is twenty-three years old. She walks away from her husband and child. She is alone in an expanse of red dirt and scrub. Carrying the toilet roll, her ears begin to tune in to the small sounds of the scrub, its dry crackles and rustlings. She hears the bell-like call of a bird she's never heard before, with its deliciously clear falling notes. There is little to hide behind in this low scrub, so she keeps walking out in a line perpendicular to the road, looking for a screen, even though there are no other cars on the road and it seems unlikely there ever will be.

Evan is calling to her from the other side of the car, standing up, calling across the roof: 'Don't go too far!' But she ignores him.

She crouches behind a waist-high wattle. Crouched there, with its sharp dry twigs in her face, she discovers that the four-note bird call goes in time with the phrase: *Have a good shit! Have a good shit!* This is her own thought, one that she need not share with her husband, whose own bowels, bound up by processed cheese, cannot be released. This is a moment of triumph, of enjoyment of one's own company, one's own body. It is relief, it is divestment, it is a small holiday. She listens to the bird and secretly names it the shit bird: *Birdus shittus*.

Linda Johnson crouches behind the partly see-through shrub, divesting herself. As she stands and rearranges her skirt, a sense of elation and wellbeing sweeps over her. She steps away, leaving a part of herself on the ground, and walks back to the car, eagerly. Red dust seeps into the tiny creases in her white leather sandals. She doesn't realise it, but her eyes are shining, her lips are smiling, but inwards, at her own joke. Evan sees this unfathomable look and smiles too, trying to catch her eye. They say nothing as he starts the car, each looking at the road ahead.

Linda has just completed a successful *dump and erase*. It's a phrase Evan will come to know well during his tracking station years. As a spacecraft orbits the earth, it will gather long lists of numbers, more every second, too many to hold inside its primitive brain. The solution is to periodically wipe the slate clean so that it can gather new lists of numbers. The request goes out, in spacecraft-speak, for permission to dump and erase. 'Yes,' whispers Evan to the spacecraft, 'you may.' And the spacecraft delivers its load, dumps all of its numbers into the eager Dish below and moves on, clean and refreshed. And then, like the attendants who once analysed every bowel movement of the Dauphin, the technicians will analyse these figures before putting them carefully away. Like the pages of French copperplate, they are with us still.

Linda Johnson looks out at the pink road and big blue sky. Her mother, Agnes, used to stop what she was doing and stand still for moments at a time. She might be chopping carrots or wiping dishes. Linda would see the blankness come over her mother's face, this strange suspended animation. And then her mother would look at the half-chopped carrot as if seeing it for the first time, as if wondering what on earth it could be. Then, if you kept watching, you might see the moment of transition as recognition dawned and Agnes reanimated. This was like water soaking into a dry sponge, making it flexible again. It made her father talk. He talked and talked, as if by talking he might be able to come to the bottom of it. With Agnes sitting quietly in a corner, smiling vaguely, he would declaim to a room full of other declaiming men all gathered around the kitchen table. They would smoke and talk and drink the strong coffee that Agnes was always heating on the stove.

At school, Linda learned that her father was a commo, her mother a reffo – a double misfortune. Children whispered that her parents were spies. She was left sitting alone on a school bench in smelling distance of the rubbish bin. She watched how other girls casually approached a skipping game, their bodies already subtly moving in time, the effortless way they moved in over the rope, not missing a beat. The playground filled and emptied, leaving Linda sitting on her bench as though stuck to it. She decided to read books and pretend she didn't care. She read boys' books out of the library: *Treasure Island* and *Robinson Crusoe* and *Ivanhoe*, full of adventure and carelessness. She realised she was enjoying her books. Maybe she *really* didn't care.

Exactly at this point, when they sensed that Linda didn't care, a little group of girls approached Linda, encouraging her to come out into the playground under their protection. Linda played this card cautiously. She shook her head and stuck to her reading for a time, making herself the aloof cat that someone wants to pat. She let them coax and coax her. And then, just at the right moment, she agreed. Having studied the moves carefully, she blended easily into the skipping game, jumping up and down to the rhythms of the rope.

All this time, there had been another girl on the far end of the same bench where Linda had sat; a plump girl with psoriasis and uncombed hair. It hadn't occurred to either of them to form a *salon des refuses*. Each had eyes only on the main game in front of them; each struggled with her exclusion alone. But now Linda was conscious, as she swayed her body in front of the rope, waiting for exactly the moment to run in and jump, that the girl with cracked and bubbling skin was sitting on the bench watching *her*.

Linda studied how normal people lived. They seemed to like tennis and other light-hearted pastimes, and if she wanted to fit in, she would do well to learn them. Her parents were of limited use in this regard: her mother was weighed down by the death of most of her relatives in the war and her father was always out at party meetings. So Linda became an autodidact, guiding her own education in tennis, doubles bridge and the best way to cut up a Queensland Blue pumpkin.

Linda got very good at Normal and even began to surpass the usual benchmarks. Like Indian families more British than British, she was more normal than normal. She conducted friendships outdoors and in public places and other people's homes. It was not that she was ashamed of her parents, it was just that their sadness and fierceness would get her nowhere in the life she wanted to join. At nineteen, she played tennis in a pair of frilly knickers that she had made from a pattern. Her short white skirt would flip up to reveal them when she stretched and twisted. This caught the eye of Evan Johnson, who blushed to the roots of his already-endangered hair. Linda walked boldly towards him, ignoring his discomfort. She seized the opportunity to wriggle away from the claws of Tragedy and History.

31

She has dumped. Her leavings sit in a small mound behind the see-through acacia bush, garnished with pink toilet paper, under the enormous silence of a perfectly blue sky. Now, she is preparing to erase.

They come unexpectedly upon a sign promising refreshments half a mile down the road. Spirits rise. They pull in at the corrugated-iron roadhouse softened by a massive purple bougainvillea and leggy geraniums in cement tubs. A thin boy with jug ears comes out to fill the car with petrol and squeegee the smashed insects across the windscreen. Rivulets of red water flee from the black rubber strip. Evan, always alive to how things work, notes the sound of a diesel generator. He goes over to look at it, stretching his arms and legs.

Linda takes Jo to the toilet, and then to see the galah in a cage under a small tree. There is a cuttlefish wedged into the wire just above the level of the bird's head. As they approach the cage, Linda begins to sing: *Dance, cocky, dance!* The galah looks at her and looks at Jo but continues to stand still, its beak open. It briefly lifts its white crest up and down in lieu of a dance. Jo studies the green and white droppings on the bottom of the cage, the sunflower seed husks, the beak marks in the cuttlebone. She will immediately forget all of this, but Linda won't, because it is part of the story of her new life.

It is dark inside, after the glare. A bottle opener is tied to a long grubby knotted string that disappears behind the laminated counter. Paper drinking straws with faded red and blue helix stripes stand tall in a metal cylinder.

'Warm for winter,' says the boy as he takes Evan's money. The till throws itself open with a thwack and a ting.

'It is warm,' says Evan.

'It's hot!' says Linda. 'We've just come from Melbourne, where it's absolutely freezing, so for us this is just like the middle of summer!'

The boy glances at Linda and looks away. She is glossy and magnificent, like a racehorse.

'Heading for the poor?' the boy asks of Evan.

Evan and Linda look at him. Then Evan remembers something he has been told – that the locals refer to Port Badminton, their destination, as the Port.

'Yes, we're off to the Port,' says Evan.

'Holiday?'

'To live.'

The boy and Evan leave it at that. Both are sparing with words. On the front cover of *The Lucky Country* there's a painting by Albert Tucker of a man with a beer in his hand, an ace of spades in his pocket, sun and sea and sail behind him, his mouth shut because all of this speaks for itself.

'Ice-cream,' says Jo, just as they are about to step back out through the plastic strips in the doorway. These are the only words she needs to use. She can stand back now and watch them take effect.

Evan would like to get going, but he can see that an ice-cream is only fair.

He gets his wallet out again, and the roadhouse boy slides the milky-coloured plastic to one side, revealing two metal tubs of ice-cream, one creamy white, the other pink.

He dips the scoop into a metal milkshake cup and flicks the water off it, awaiting further instructions.

'Strawberry or vanilla?' asks Linda, but these words go over Jo's head. Evan holds her up over the icy, vaporous tubs so she can see in. 'That one, or that one?'

'That one.'

Out in the sun, Evan and Linda suck their fizzy drinks through straws, monitoring Jo's progress with her ice-cream. It is melting in the sun, streams of pink running down both hands to the elbows.

'Let me neaten it off for you,' says Evan. He hands Linda his drink and takes the ice-cream from Jo. He stands there in the sun, licking expertly around the edges, getting rid of the melted stuff, leaving a core of the hard stuff.

It was just as Donald Horne described it in *The Lucky Country*: 'The image of Australia is of a man in an open-necked shirt solemnly enjoying an ice-cream. His kiddy is beside him.'

Evan is back at the wheel, the motor running as he waits for Linda to reinstall a mopped-down Jo. At this moment, Evan Johnson has five years, twenty weeks, thirteen hours, nine minutes and approximately twenty-two seconds to live. When he suddenly disappears, presumed dead, he will leave a whole neat drawer of long socks, all matched impotently to their mates, never again to be animated by his purposeful feet.

Linda gets in and slams her door. Evan's right foot, in its sweaty sock, in its humid shoe, presses down on the accelerator.

THREE

Stolen

As Evan Johnson was pressing down on the accelerator, trying to speed up time, I was sitting listlessly in my cage in Clam Street. Time had slowed to a barely moving thing. I sat, and nothing happened. I inched sideways up my perch and sat there. Nothing happened. I inched back the other way. I hooked my claws into the wire and screamed. Nobody came out to see why. I didn't know, then, that it was five years, twenty weeks, thirteen hours, nine minutes and approximately twenty-two seconds to Liberation. Evan Johnson would fall, and I would rise.

Falling man, rising bird.

I can barely remember how I came to be trapped in the cage at the Kellys'. The memories come in a series of images, of feelings, of darkness and rocking. They grew stronger after I saw a picture in the *Australasian Bird Fancier*. I was reading over Lizzie's shoulder – from her shoulder, that is – when we spotted a colour photograph of a baby galah.

It was a tiny thing of translucent pink and grey skin, enormous bluish eye bulges and flipper-like wing buds.

It was stuck all over with the quills that would become feathers. After a moment, Lizzie tried to turn the page, but I beaked my way down her arm and put my claw out to stop her. I needed to look for longer, to imagine myself as a baby; to weep for myself.

I was sure I could remember my earliest days, nestled with my siblings in our hole in the gum tree on the bank of Chinaman's Pool. We squabbled, elbowed each other, fell asleep and woke up as we waited for our parents to return and feed us. We were one mass of tiny birds, only just beginning to differentiate, to express our various personalities. We were learning how to surprise each other; how to laugh and engage in basic slapstick.

And then a human hand reached in, making exploratory movements to the left and right. We had never seen such a thing before. We were so surprised that we simply sat there like idiots, gaping. The fingers passed over my siblings and closed over me.

I was dropped headfirst into a shirt pocket. I could hear the roar and thump of the giant beating heart underneath it. The hand held the opening of the pocket closed. Thus, I was borne away in darkness from Chinaman's Pool.

My foster parent was a skinny barefoot nine-year-old boy who rarely went to school. You could see his rib cage, you could hear the rumblings in his stomach. He hand-raised me, pushing bits of bread and water into my beak. I loved these meals, the gentleness with which they were administered. I began to fall in love with him. We played gentle little games. Under his care, I grew quickly. My feathers came through. One day he told me I had to raise enough money for a pie. He said if I wasn't sold, he might have to make *me* into a pie. He would have to pluck me and chop me up into little pieces and put me in the oven in a pastry case. When I screamed he said, 'Shoosh, I'm only joking.'

But he was serious about selling me on. He put me in a splintery wooden box with narrow-gauge chicken wire nailed over the top of it, and knocked on doors. I was peered at and admired, but it wasn't until we arrived at Kevin Kelly's blue house in Clam Street that genuine interest was expressed.

Little fingers came in through the chicken wire like waving sea anemones. I nipped at them, drawing blood. 'What did I tell you?' bellowed a gingery man. 'Bitey!'

I was moved into a larger wire cage, the one I was to inhabit for the duration of my life with the Kellys. This cage was about two feet by two feet wide and about two and a half feet tall. As I grew to full size, I found I did not have quite enough room to completely stretch out my wings.

My meals were all the same; mixed seed poured into my tin dish. Mrs Kelly barely looked at me as she cleaned my dishes; she wore the same expression as she did when watering the garden or pegging the clothes out on the line.

At the bottom of my cage there was a metal tray to collect my droppings. This would occasionally be removed and hosed out. At these times, I'd enjoy some time on the patchy grass of the Kelly backyard. I'd feel the spray from the hose and get a good view of the sky.

Every day, sometimes for hours on end, I called out to my bird flock. It was a double chirrup, the double chirrup that means:

Where are you?

I'm here!

Wait for me!

Over here!

Over here!

I'm not sure exactly what I was hoping for. Did I think my brothers and sisters were in those flocks? My parents? Did I think they would sneak up to my cage in the dead of night, unhook my little latch and take me with them? I don't think I knew in any detail; I just wanted release and relief, and that pink and grey flock represented it.

But they couldn't hear me. They were flying too high, too fast.

I paced up and down on my perch. Trapped. Forgotten.

And then a boy of about my age landed on the fence. It was a quiet interlude; the Kellys were all indoors, perhaps having an afternoon nap or playing cards.

We began to chat, he from the fence, me from my cage.

He came back from time to time. Eventually he told me, shyly, that he was looking for a girlfriend.

I asked him to come over and inspect my latch. He looked over his shoulder, this way and that. The coast was clear. He landed on my cage in a sudden, exhilarating movement. Just inches away from my face, the pink and grey feathers, a beating heart. I could see the individual pink feathers under his eyes; the expressive arch of white feathers in his crest.

40

I vibrated with flock-feeling. The flying muscles in my shoulders began to pull. I felt the urgency and possibility. The young galah looked at the latch first with one eye, and then turned his head and looked with the other. He beaked it, tested it with his tongue, brought a claw up to it.

'This is easy,' he said, and flicked the little hook. The door swung open.

And then there was the swish and thwack of the screen door, and Mr Kelly came through it. I froze where I was on the perch, one claw up, one wing out, as if in a game of statues.

'Marj! Come and have a look at this!'

Marj took a moment to appear, tea towel in hand, a slight frown.

'What?'

'Look at the cage.'

Marj approached, not seeing.

'It's been unlatched,' said Mr Kelly. 'A wild galah unlatched it! I saw it fly off!'

'Are you sure you didn't just leave it open?' said Mrs Kelly. 'When you did the water?'

'No, I'm saying I saw a wild galah unlatching the door of the cage.'

'One of the kids probably did it,' said Mrs Kelly. 'A wild galah wouldn't do that.'

'I *saw* it, Marj!' Mr Kelly insisted.

Small children appeared.

'Cocky nearly flew away,' Kevin Kelly told them.

The children began to cry. By now I was *theirs*, and they did not like to lose things.

41

'You've got to clip the wing, Kev,' said Mrs Kelly.

Kevin Kelly relatched my cage.

Clip the wing. It didn't sound good.

Kevin Kelly pins me down top of the ironing board. I struggle and writhe.

'Hold it down *properly*, Kev,' says Mrs Kelly.

His big strong hands press down. He could easily kill me but is choosing not to. I stare up at him with one eye. He seems sympathetic, but he is doing what he is told. Mrs Kelly's dressmaking scissors come in for a short, sharp snip. I scream my death scream. It comes from deep inside; like my chirruping call to galahs flying overhead, it surprises me, this voice made of pure instinct. I hear a wailing chorus from the children outside the door. They are crying for me. As soon as he releases the pressure, I latch on to Kevin Kelly's big meaty thumb.

Back in the cage, I crooned over myself. I sat miserably in a corner, refusing to eat or dance. This went on for an age, or perhaps only twenty minutes. I was a very young galah, and easily distracted. As consolation, I was given a cuttlebone. My beak sank into the silky, pleasantly resistant substance. The children were paying more attention to me: they, too, had felt the punishing hands of Mr and Mrs Kelly. I had gained sibling status.

And Mr Kelly planted sunflowers for me.

I heard my name mentioned as he dropped seeds into the ground and watered them in. At first they were too small for me to see, but I watched as the children and Mr Kelly hunkered down around them, discussing the tiny twin leaves that had appeared above the ground. They grew quickly in the Port Badminton sunshine and cold water from the tap in the kitchen. They were giants, like Jack's beanstalk. Finally, against the sky, the translucent yellow petals. The Kellys admired them and, as they discussed them, they kept mentioning my name.

Slowly, they withered and died. The black seeds sloughed off their fuzz, revealing themselves in a dazzling spiral.

'It's nearly time to give the seeds to the cocky,' said Mr Kelly one day.

I danced eagerly, greedy and impatient.

But nothing happened. I screeched for hours, nobody knew why, and I couldn't explain. I said, in a raspy dry little voice, 'Cocky want a drink' and 'Dance, cocky, dance'. I used every phrase, every sentence, in my repertoire. I couldn't find the magic key, the word that would open the door to the experience I craved. I screamed blue murder.

And then, one day, it happened. My patience had paid off. I sat calmly, quivering only slightly as they pushed pieces of the giant seed head in through the little gate in my cage. I gorged. I steadied the piece of sunflower head in one claw and dipped my beak in among the black seeds packed closely together. I nuzzled into them, picking them out one by one, rubbing the shells between upper and lower beak until they cracked and the grey inner seed emerged onto my tongue. I swallowed down and then dipped in again. I did this, systematically, until the bottom of the cage was a carpet of spent cartridges. I felt ill, but I still eyed off the remaining heads on the old table near the back door.

'She loves it, doesn't she?'

And then I saw him. The wild young galah.

He was sitting on the fence with his girlfriend, casually, as if nothing were amiss.

I screeched in rage. The girlfriend rolled her eyes and flew off, out of sight. I could hear her calling him, telling him to hurry up.

I quieted down and looked at him. He was handsome, bursting with flight and possibility. He looked at me, wordlessly. *If things had been different . . .*

I would like to say that I was fully present to this moment; that I inhabited the grief and sadness; that I said a dignified goodbye. The fact is, I was waiting for him to leave so that I could quell my stabbing jealousy and rage by tearing into the seed head. I gorged until I'd eaten everything in the cage and then screamed for more. It was only later, looking back, that the sadness welled up and became almost unbearable.

I was now, truly, a caged galah, a pet. It was easier to choose not to hear the exuberant calls of the flock. I began to lose the language of my birth and to think in English. I learned it along with my new little human flock. From babble to simple commands to whole sentences; experimental applications of the rules of grammatical structure. These sentences began to run together, to become richer, capable of being deployed to beg, to taunt, to entertain. During daylight hours, the yard was a scene of constant vocalisation and movement: calling, shrieking, fighting, flailing, flushing. I was on a permanent campaign to make them notice me, to join in.

Sometimes Kevin Kelly would scratch me behind the ear. I'd enjoy it for a moment, purring like a cat, and then sink my beak into his big wide finger.

I couldn't help it. I'd bite before I knew what I was doing. I'd bite out of excitement, joy, neediness, desperate attention-seeking. I soon had a poor reputation.

'It bites,' the Kellys would warn visitors.

As a biter, I was shunned. Shunned, I became dull and sometimes irritating company.

I wasn't happy, but I got used to it. I sat in my cage and watched the Kelly family and its attendant relatives and neighbours. There were nicely dressed ladies, some wearing perfume, who hurried across the yard to the toilet. In time I understood that these were Mrs Kelly's customers; she was making dresses for them.

Every now and then the lazy ginger cat would absent-mindedly rub itself on the corner of my cage. I'd stealthily stretch out a claw and squeeze its tail. The cat would jump and hiss. I found this hilarious. I was always looking for the cat, hoping it would come my way.

At dawn, sometimes, I'd catch a whiff of a smell that reminded me of the eucalypt I was born in.

I'd watch the moon rise from over the back fence, behind a tree, and then clear the tree. Then it would disappear behind the roofline of the back verandah, leaving just moonlight. Sometimes the Kellys stood out in the backyard, not far from my cage, and discussed the moon. There would be three or four people of different sizes and a caged galah, looking up at the moon together. They said a man was going to walk on the moon. That's why there was a Dish.

A dish, a moon, a spoon. I misunderstood most of what I heard.

The Kellys would all go back inside the house, the screen door closing with a little *thwip*. I'd think about the moon. I imagined a man hanging on to the side of the moon as it rose in the sky. The surface looked slippery; I couldn't see how his feet could possibly get a grip.

And then I'd prepare for bed by turning my face back over my body, nestling my beak into my own feathers. And sleep.

***

Lizzie tried again to turn the page. I nipped her on the hand. She said: 'Stop it, you little mongrel,' and swept me roughly off the magazine so that I toppled onto the floor.

I sulked, waddling across the floor, climbing up my perch. I muttered angrily, in words and phrases that had the rhythm and vowel sounds of cussing and swearing, if not the correct dentition.

I continued my reverie, my brooding.

***

I began to take an interest in stories. Perhaps this was a genetic, instinctual trait: galahs are consummate storytellers, playful and freewheeling. They embellish, exaggerate, play for laughs. Sitting alone in my cage at the Kellys', I knew nothing of this tradition, but I found myself leaning forward, listening closely, when the children – my new siblings – began to tell tales. For example:

'Mum, Susan put her pants on her head.'

'Did not!'

'Did so!'

'Stop it, you two.'

'But, Mum! Susan put her *pants* on her *head*!'

I can see – now – that this is not a particularly good story. But to a young galah there were possibilities. The imagination fired. Yes, a child would look very funny with its pants on its head! I screamed with laughter. *Pants! Head!* I hung upside down in my cage and screeched, throwing my head from side to side. If I'd had tears in my eyes they would have been running down my face and onto the floor of the cage, to be soaked up in the dry newspaper there. If I'd had arms I'd have been clutching them at my sides from laughing so hard. I screeched until they all turned to me and said, 'Shut up, cocky!'

And I said, 'Shut up, cocky!'

And they all thought that was funny. This was how I *joined in*.

I wanted to tell stories of my own. I wanted an audience, a listener, someone. But there was a problem in transmission. I could think them up, but I could not make myself understood.

I would become despondent, but I never quite gave up.

I made up stories, kept them in my mind, went over them, improved them.

I worked with the material at hand. I studied the geraniums and vinca in the foreground and the riot of purple bougainvillea in the distance, beyond the toilet. At night, insects would gather around the dim light bulb on the back verandah if it was left on by mistake. The cat, wide awake through the night, might arrive with a rabbit or a rat. The sunflowers. The arrival of the second-hand electric twin-tub washing machine that turned Mrs Kelly's life around. The garden hose spraying water in a great glittering arc. Oh, how I loved that water! Sometimes on a sweltering day I'd be carried out, cage and all, to a spot of scraggly dry grass in the backyard to be hosed lightly in a fine spray. Most of all there was the toilet, and the to-ing and fro-ing. Eventually someone would appear for a toilet run. They might be in there for a brief time or a long time. Others might gather at the door, banging on it, pleading or demanding.

'Hurry up! I've got to *go*!'

There might be a small, miserable reply.

'I *can't*.'

I pieced together information about the world beyond the yard – places like School and Down the Street – through repeated phrases and fragments of story.

'I'm just going Down the Street. Anyone want to come?'

Or:

'Stop it now. You have to go to School.'

'No!'

'Do you want a smack on the bottom?'

Down the Street was popular; School unpopular.

At the mention of Down the Street they'd all come running out the back door and disappear around the side of the house. There would be the sound of a car engine firing up – or quite often the sound of an engine desperately turning over but failing to ignite – and then the deep silence that would ensue once all Kellys were off the premises.

Then, without the noise, I could hear it: the sound of the galah flock in the distance. An aching, painful, aerial sound. I would block it by shrieking, by thinking, by flapping. I preferred not to listen.

Then they'd all be back. They'd have milk and bread and sometimes prizes like a tin of sweetened condensed milk or little white bags of mixed lollies to be savoured but also fought over and cried over, sometimes in front of me.

I started small with my stories. *The cat is walking on the moon with its pants on its head.* Or: *The washing machine is biting the buttons off all the school shirts.*

Then I began to develop my ideas.

The bougainvillea rustles out of the yard in the middle of the night and goes down the main street of town. It rustles right down the main street, dropping its papery purple flowers all the way, and comes back before dawn. The bougainvillea comes back with milk and bread held in its branches. It holds them there greedily, hiding them under its flowers and leaves, not eating or drinking them, until the bread goes hard and stale and the milk goes yellow and smelly. Two weeks later a boy finds them and says, 'What's this bread and milk doing in the bougainvillea?!' He looks bamboozled. He has the look of a

cartoon character with a great big question mark over his head.
The end.

Are you laughing? Well, probably not. But it was one of my earliest stories, and I'm fond of it. You can see that I'm beginning to sustain a narrative, to get movement on the page, to explore the idea of puzzlement.

I told myself stories, lots of funny stories. I laughed to myself a lot. Sometimes I'd make myself weep. I'd spend days crafting something elegant, something funny, something snaking this way and that, doubling back on itself like a galah in flight, something to make you wonder, something to stop time, something to pass time, something to make you sit beside my cage, spellbound. I had the story, I was bursting to tell it, but I had no way to tell it. I'd have the words on the tip of my bulbous tongue, but when I opened my beak, all I could say was:

Dance, cocky, dance!

or

Cocky want a drink?

or

Hello, cocky!

or

Shut up, cocky!

That's when I'd scream in frustration. There was no greater frustration than that. I'd have the funniest, wittiest, cutest little story – and no way to tell it.

When I finally saw Down the Street and School, I was amazed. They were nothing like what I had imagined. Down the Street was altogether less vivid. There were no great vats holding lollies, no camels carrying monkeys on their backs, no aeroplanes landing on the tarmac. School was surrounded by a low fence, easily scaled by any child; the gate at the front was easily unlatched. Any child could have escaped at will.

The Sea, by contrast, was more powerful, more dazzling, than anything I had imagined. I saw it on my second walk with Lizzie. The glittering Indian Ocean. This was Kevin Kelly's realm, and he had barely mentioned it in all those years. We went out again at sunset, when the sky over the dark sea was lit up in pink and orange and grey. I almost swooned off Lizzie's shoulder.

It was on Lizzie's shoulder, as we made our way about town, that I was able to reconnect – to some extent – with my galah colleagues, wild and caged. We could shout a few words to each other as Lizzie and I passed under the gum tree near the post office where galahs liked to land and gossip; we'd stop to talk to a pet galah in a cage on a front verandah.

These connections are transient, and bittersweet. Among wild galahs I find teenage tales about who is pairing off with whom of little interest; older galahs become impatient with my blank stares when they discuss the merits of different types of hollows in mature eucalypts or hilarious prickle feasts on the town oval. Pet galahs can be narrow, depressive and incurious. I try to talk about my reading, or test my stories, but these topics fall flat. Still, there is something to be said for these remnants of pink and grey company. They remind me: I am a bird.

***

Lizzie comes wheedling back to me making little kissing noises, holding out a bony finger to scratch me under the ear. I give in, and soon we are back at the table eating biscuits and drinking tea. I understand, all over again, how lucky I am.

FOUR

The wooden salad bowl

LINDA AND EVAN had studied the place, Port Badminton, in Evan's old school atlas. They'd looked at how Shark Bay jutted out halfway up the west side of the continent; at how the town was just a tiny speck surrounded by nothing but outback on one side and the Indian Ocean on the other. It would always be warm there, at that latitude.

On the day of the interview, Linda rang Evan's office to say he was sick and would not be coming in. Evan took the tram across town, feeling hot and uncomfortable in the same suit he had worn for his wedding. When he was shown into the interview room, he saw immediately that he was overdressed. The two men opposite him were wearing open-necked shirts, their sleeves rolled up. It seemed Evan had caught these men mid-stream in a discussion that had begun some time before. They looked up, stood, and shook hands. Then they sat down and resumed their conversation. Evan, assuming they were waiting for someone else, a third interviewer perhaps, joined the discussion. He was still waiting for the interview to begin when he realised it had ended and that he was being ushered out. Afterwards, he stood on the street for a moment, wondering whether it had gone well or badly, not knowing whether to feel one thing or another.

When he got home, Linda zeroed in on the problem of the suit and the interview's inconclusive start and finish, and decided it was hopeless. She even cried about it, because the idea of Port Badminton had begun to grow on her. Then, believing it was hopeless, she turned her mind to other things. She had almost completely forgotten about Port Badminton when she found an envelope – On Her Majesty's Service – in the letterbox. She put it in the middle of the table.

Glancing at the envelope as the afternoon wore on, she allowed herself little rills of hope. At four o'clock she put a small vase of flowers next to it, to dramatise it. Then she held it up to the light, hoping to read through the paper. Yes or no? Heads or tails? Here or there? But it was opaque.

The answer, of course, was yes. Good fortune was smiling on Evan Johnson, a man who happened to be in the right place at the right time with an ideal set of technical skills. Had he been born twenty years earlier, he might have been presented with different challenges: being shot at over the sea in a fighter plane, for example, or trying to survive a Japanese prisoner-of-war camp.

Instead, he was being offered the perfect job for a man of his interests and abilities, for which he would be paid handsomely. He bought a brand-new blue EH Holden station wagon and, on the same day, drove Linda and little

Jo to a department store, where they selected a complete set of modern, light pieces of furniture that could easily be packed and sent ahead. They sold or gave away their dark, heavy, second-hand things.

The miles on the posts have all been consumed. The Johnsons have arrived exactly thirty minutes after their Estimated Time of Arrival. They get out of the car in front of their new house in Clam Street, slightly wobbly on land. Evan lifts the lid of the new letterbox beside the front gate. Inside, as expected, there is an envelope, and inside that, a brass key. 'Look at your new house, Jo!' says Linda. And Evan says: 'Everything is all set. It's all working like a charm.'

Children in pyjamas run out of a house further down the street, shrieking, 'They're here! They're here!' only to disappear again.

The Johnsons mount the stairs to their front door. It swings open, easily, on oiled hinges. In the brand-new kitchen – the smell of newness still rising from surfaces – Evan and Linda find a childishly rendered WELCOME sign hanging from string. The refrigerator is on and purring. There is an electric jug on the bench, and teacups and saucers. There is a note written by the wife of one of Evan's colleagues. This is an invitation to a welcoming barbecue tomorrow night. *But we won't disturb you tonight – we'll let you settle in!*

Evan shuts himself into the toilet while Linda and Jo run up and down the length of the house, opening doors, looking into rooms, all of which already have some useful furniture in them. Cold, struggling Melbourne, dark heavy furniture, woolly coats, itchy stockings all seem a long way away. Watched by Linda, Jo runs into Evan's arms when he reappears in the kitchen after a triumphant flush of the toilet. They all do a little jig, even though Evan normally doesn't dance.

The next morning, a twelve-seater van turns up in front of the house to collect Evan for work. Linda and Jo stand near the letterbox as Evan hops in. He is wearing a new pair of long white socks, unleashed just that morning from their cellophane packet. Through the van's windows Linda can see him shaking hands with the other men. They wave briefly to Linda or nod their heads. Linda and Jo stand beside the letterbox, watching until the van disappears from view.

In the van, Evan eagerly joins the banter, signing up on the spot for the Trackers, their own basketball team. Like Evan, some of these men are wearing horn-rimmed glasses in the style of Donald Horne himself, as seen in the author photograph on the back cover of *The Lucky Country*. All, including the driver, are wearing shorts and polished shoes and long socks.

Evan Johnson is given a place at a console and handed a set of bulbous earphones. There are banks of lights and switches to get on top of. He learns how to send instructions and receive information from passing spacecraft. He learns the first of the dozens of acronyms that will play through his mind in waking and sleeping hours for the rest of his life. He learns when to listen and when to speak. At the end of the day, when work is done, he switches his mind to beer and perhaps fishing. After that, to home and family.

In the morning, after breakfast, the van appears to herald a new day of absorbing, enjoyable activities.

While Evan learns the ropes at the tracking station, Linda Johnson makes her first public appearance in the town of Port Badminton. She emerges from the driver's seat of the EH Holden and opens the back door for Jo. Shopkeepers, other housewives and the local dogger in his dirty Land Rover watch her openly. This is not only because Linda is tall and striking; it is also because she is new in town and every new person must be thoroughly scrutinised. The stares seem hard and long; it is hard to tell whether they are simply curious or vaguely hostile.

When she goes into the butcher's shop, the butcher addresses her as Mrs Johnson. She is surprised that he knows her name. He knows that Evan is working at the tracking station on Red Range. He knows that Evan is picked up each morning in a van, along with his colleagues, giving Linda daytime use of the family car for shopping and errands. The butcher watches as Jo toddles out through the glass door in her white sandals and puffy dress. Her Melbourne skin seems dangerously white and delicate.

Out on the street, Jo is startled by a grown woman sitting in the doorway next door to the butcher's. Their faces are at about the same height. The woman says, 'Hello, little one.' Jo shrinks shyly into her mother's skirts. As they walk away, Jo asks loudly, 'Why is that lady sitting on the ground?'

Linda grabs her arm and says, 'Shh.' The dogger, who has been watching from the open doorway of his Land Rover, calls out, 'Stay away from the Abos, kid.' Linda ignores him but feels his eyes on her back.

The woman in the doorway watches, too. The little girl is like a soft white grub, an easy snack for an omnivorous bird.

With Jo down for an afternoon nap, Linda takes her time unpacking boxes. She unwraps plates and cups and puts them away in pristine cupboards. There is room for everything; there is even space around things. The house is a blank slate; she can decorate it exactly as she pleases in clean, modern lines. She imagines the things she would like.

There is little to be found in the local shops, so over the following weeks she pores over department store catalogues and receives things in the mail, including a wooden salad bowl and matching servers. A women's magazine recommends *crisp vegetables seasoned with garlic, oil, tarragon vinegar and freshly ground pepper*. She toys with the idea of growing tarragon in a pot near the back door.

***

With some exceptions – the bank, the post office, a couple of churches – Port Badminton was not then a town of brick or solid stone. It had a feeling of temporariness about it, as if it could easily be washed away in a flood or blown away by a cyclone. It was held together with cable and rope and a few banged-in nails. Something was always being tied or untied, lashed or unlashed, battened down or loosened off. It was a town of demountable classrooms and clinics. Small homes might be brought in – whole or partly disman- tled – on the back of a truck.

Every couple of years – as now – the lines of the western edge of the town changed shape as tonnes of silt were dumped at the mangrove-covered delta. The seawall at the bottom of the main street was an attempt to fix at least this part of it in place. It was planted along the top with date palms, some say by the Afghan cameleers who brought the wool in from the interior. They'd drive the teams down the main street and turn right into Dromedary Lane. The wool was then piled onto a train that clacked along its tracks from town, over the swampy delta, all the way out to the end of the One Mile Jetty and into the maws of ships. By the early 1960s, the ships had stopped coming and the jetty was given over exclusively to fishing. The fish were teeming. You could always get yourself dinner, if you had a hook and a line.

Port Badminton was the perfect habitat for men who wanted to rig something up, give something a burl, have a go. Or simply to escape problems that had accumulated in cities thousands of miles away. One could sleep in one's car on the side of the road, or out on the beach under the stars, or in the long grass on the riverbank, free of interference. One could use the things of the earth – the trees, the sea, the rocks – and combine them with rope and engines and lengths of tarpaulin to create something that might work, even if only for a little while, until ropes frayed or metal rusted in the salt air. And if it didn't work or didn't go, no harm done. You could always give it another go. There was all the time in the world.

It was an ideal habitat for the sort of man Donald Horne calls the *practical Australian*. The practical Australian does not concern himself with the big picture; he likes to get on with *a bit of detail*.

Mrs Lillian O'Donoghue, postmistress at Hamelin Pool on the bottom lip of Shark Bay, is roused out of bed in the middle of the night. The elderly Mrs O'Donoghue shuffles into her slippers, throws a dressing-gown over her nightgown and calls out, 'Coming!' A bespectacled man in pressed shorts and long socks is standing at her door. There are astronauts in space, orbiting the earth, practicing docking manoeuvres. They're outside their craft, vulnerable as witchetty grubs, depending for communications on a single wire running along the top of sheep fences. There has been a lightning strike. Everything has gone dead. Can she help?

Mrs O'Donoghue swings into action. She fires up the old telegraph. They're going to have to do this the old way, using Morse code. Her mind may have forgotten, but her fingers have not. They fly over the keys, giving coordinates and other vital evidence of life and progress. She does this continuously for three hours. She is brought cups of tea. At 3 am, men from the Postmaster-General's office arrive at the break in the line and fix it. Mrs O'Donoghue goes back to bed.

*

Everyone loves these stories: they like the invigorating contrast between high technology and bush improvisations. These are the stories the trackers love to tell, over the years, at barbecues.

Another concerns Port Badminton's Great Sanitary Towel Shortage. There were no sanitary towels to be had, not at the chemist, not at Wesfarmers. Bleeding women were left to improvise – to return to earlier methods involving boiled rags hung out to dry (as discreetly as possible) under the hygienic Port Badminton sun.

Only later, much later, did the reason for this shortage emerge: the absorbent, lint-free sanitary pads were perfectly suited to cleaning newly installed wave-guide pipes. Once the technicians ran out of cotton waste, they moved on to other materials to hand in the town of Port Badminton.

***

Evan and his colleagues are walking out along the One Mile Jetty at dawn, carrying fishing gear. Their guest is NASA's Number Three Engineer from Houston, Texas. Their conversation encompasses Work and Leisure but rarely Romance, Politics or Philosophy (these are Donald Horne's *practical* men). With the best possible work and the best possible leisure, these men are enjoying themselves immensely. In fact, they find it hard to imagine anything better than what they have. They follow the rail tracks of the discontinued steam train, explaining to each other what they know of the jetty's origins and specifications. The first half of the walk is over the silty mud, and then they're out over the water proper, listening to it slap satisfyingly at the great wooden pylons. The sun rises, gradually lighting the Indian Ocean, deepening its blue-green hue.

The mulloway – also known as kingies, giant plump fish taller than an eight-year-old child – are milling about as if waiting for the hook. The Number Three Engineer almost immediately catches one, bringing its large silver body over the railing to gasp and flip on the old wooden planks of the jetty. They eat it that night at a barbecue at Evan Johnson's house, where his beautiful long-legged wife serves salad – sadly there is not yet tarragon – from a wooden salad bowl.

Back in Houston some weeks later, the Number Three Engineer picks up the phone and calls Evan Johnson. Evan is on the other side of the planet, in a different time zone and a long, long way down the NASA food chain. But having bonded over mulloway, the two men can be free and natural with each other. (Evan's English colleagues, used to barriers of class and rank, find this remarkable.)

'We need you guys to set up a system to check radiation levels in the upper atmosphere,' says the Number Three Engineer. 'You'll need a big flat area about the size of a football field. What do you think?'

'We'll give it a burl,' says Evan.

That evening, Evan stays out at the Port Hotel until 11 pm, drinking with colleagues. (This is still a novelty for Evan: in Melbourne, the pubs close at 6 pm sharp to force working men back to their homes. In Western Australia, it is understood that the economy would grind to a halt under these conditions. In Port Badminton and other outlying regions, closing time is simply the proprietor's prerogative.)

Buying his round, Evan tells Crowie that a couple of sandhills on Red Range will need flattening.

'Right you are,' says Crowie.

As relevant customers approach the bar – someone from the Shire, someone with a bulldozer – Crowie makes the arrangements. The next day, men and machinery turn up at the appointed place. Crowie himself is there to supervise. Others who have no practical role but have expressed a desire to be *in on it* are there too. Thus, there is quite a little crowd in attendance at the flattening of the sandhills. A grader arrives to add the finishing touches, smoothing out the red sand. At day's end, Evan puts in an international call to the Number Three Engineer.

'We've done it,' says Evan.

There is a pause on the line. Evan feels the ray of approval beaming from one end of the planet to the other.

With a smaller team of men, Evan's task the next day is to lay lengths of chicken wire over the flattened red earth. The bales of wire catch the sunlight in hot little flares. The wire is hard to tame, preferring to spring back into its roll rather than lie flat on the ground. Once it has been laid out like a tablecloth and pegged in, the men erect eight tall masts at one end of the field that look like a proliferating set of Victorian Football League goalposts. At a forty-five-degree angle between the vertical masts and the horizontal chicken wire, two metal pipes are positioned to act as aerials. Strung between the masts is a latticework of copper wire held in place with guy ropes made of Dacron, a new material that is strong and rot-resistant. It is an *ionospheric listening device*. Chicken wire is now ready to listen to the universe.

The next day, a big male emu strolls out across the chicken wire, curling his toes with every step, lifting the wire out of the red earth. Evan darts out with a hessian bag and a rope. He launches himself at the emu, but it kicks and flails and within a minute rolls of chicken wire are springing up out of the red earth. One has the furious emu wrapped up in it.

After that, the trackers decide on peaceful coexistence.

They peg the chicken wire down very firmly, so that any emu can walk across with ease.

But another problem emerges. The trackers notice that the guy ropes, carefully tied off during the day, are all undone by the following morning. The copper wire is lying in the red dirt, the grubby Dacron cords lying slackly on top. It's a mystery. The men stand looking at the scene, baffled.

They reassemble and reknot, firmly.

But it's the same again the next day: an identical scene of dishevelment.

Evan Johnson volunteers to get to the bottom of it.

At the end of the day, when his colleagues leave work in the van, he stays behind. He keeps working until midnight, and then goes to bed under his desk. He rolls up tea towels from the staff kitchen to form a pillow. The floor is hard and it is impossible to sleep. At 2 am he gives up and returns to his desk to read Carter Brown's *The Myopic Mermaid*.

At 2.45 a new wave of tiredness comes over him and he returns to the floor, hopefully. At 4 am, before it is light, he makes himself a thermos of tea and a ham sandwich in the trackers' kitchen and goes outside to wait. The chicken wire is spread over the red dirt before him. The aerial is pointing out properly at forty-five degrees. The lines of copper wire are intact, held by the Dacron cord.

He nestles down behind an acacia shrub – not hiding, exactly, but sitting very quietly. He listens to the falling bell-like song of the chiming wedgebills. The locals call the bird the 'did ya get drunk?', because these words fit the rhythm. *Did ya get drunk?* Evan, listening carefully, notes that there is a fifth syllable in the call and mentally adds a new word. Now the birds are singing, *But did ya get drunk?* He intends to tell someone about the fifth syllable but he will forget, because these are predawn thoughts and, finally, in the soft red dirt, under a lightening sky, he falls asleep.

Almost immediately he is woken by a shriek. A flock of pink and grey galahs, entering stage left, takes up various positions on the guy ropes.

'Galahs,' says Evan aloud.

They squabble and chat to each other like women in a clothing factory. They busy themselves over each knot with focus and determination, as if paid by the piece.

Evan watches them quietly, making no move to intervene. He unscrews the lid of his thermos and pours himself a cup of tea, thinking about a solution. He'll splice the rope and put binding over it so the birds can't untie the knots.

Then he leaps to his feet and shoos the galahs away.

They rise up in a straggly pink and grey cloud, complaining indignantly. They haven't *finished*.

Evan assembles his tools and materials and gets to work splicing and binding. The sun rises higher and warmer. The bush begins to crackle in the heat. There are little scurryings. The chiming wedgebills fall silent; they'll pipe up again when it's cooler.

As Evan splices and binds, the myopic mermaid swims to the surface of his mind. Her silver tail flashes in the glitter of the waves. For her, the world is a beautiful watery blur. She splashes Evan playfully. He watches her greenish blonde hair fan out under the water. He tries to hold her still so that he can study the line at her belly where skin becomes scale, but she slithers out of his hands. The binding and splicing complete, Evan returns to his desk and drops down into his chair. His feet are hot in his socks and shoes. He would like to stretch out under his desk once more, but the workday is well in hand. So he gets on with a bit of detail.

When they arrive the next morning, the galahs soon realise that they have been foiled. After trying their best, they give up in disgust.

But it isn't over yet.

Next, the trackers notice that the copper wire lattice-work between the masts is breaking. Evan boards the van the next morning with a portable army stretcher, a grey blanket, a tin of sardines, a packet of ginger nut biscuits and another Carter Brown. He sleeps well this time. In the morning he discovers that the galahs, having given up on undoing knots, are now using the copper wire lattice as a gym, swinging around one wire and down to the next. They exercise themselves thus, like Ukrainian gymnasts, until the wire snaps. Then they start on another one.

The Number Three Engineer sends more copper wire, but this time with unbreakable steel at the core. The galahs are happy with their new reinforced parallel bars; the trackers are happy and, most importantly, NASA is happy.

Taking a break with a cup of instant coffee, Evan watches the galahs as they lift up and fly off to the right in a cloud of grey, then suddenly loop around in a cloud of pink and fly off into the distance, as if painting the infinity symbol against the sky. Now that a solution has been found, he can allow that they are beautiful.

***

This is how the galahs tuned the Dish. The Dish was young and impressionable at the time; it had only just been switched on. As the galahs bounced on the copper wire, signals began to pass rapidly back and forth between bird and Dish, bird and Dish. The Dish had to make a series of radical adjustments to keep up. After a few weeks of daily bouncing, the signals between Dish and galahs were crystal clear. *All* Port Badminton galahs now had the ability to send and receive, whether they had been directly involved or not. Mostly, they didn't bother to check their signals; the information was rarely relevant. But when I first rode out of Clam Street on Lizzie's shoulder and came into direct line of sight of the Dish, I felt the signals vibrating through me.

DISH: 04 11 54 48 CC Intrepid, Houston. Looks good. 04 11 54 51 CMP How's the tube, Jerry? 04 11 54 56 CC Real good, Dick. Real good. 04 11 54 58 CMP Okay. 04 11 54 59 CDR Okay, Dick. Yawing left, 60. 04 11 55 04 CMP Hey, Pete, you're cutting in and out to me. 04 11 55 07 CDR Roger.

At first I had no idea what it all meant. But then, without any effort on my part – as if I were watching a photograph developing in a bath of chemicals – the pictures formed and became clearer.

DISH: Stand by.
GALAH: Roger? Do I say Roger?
DISH: Yes. That's right.
[Pause]
GALAH: What do you want to say?
DISH: Nothing. I'm bored. I'm going over some old material.
GALAH: Roger that.

I, too, like to go over old material. To repeat it, try to make sense of it, see it from another angle.

This sideline in galah communication didn't affect the Dish's performance in the main game, of course. In fact, it may have enhanced it in ways not yet understood by science.

***

Jo Johnson is sitting on the polished wooden floor with a pile of coloured wooden blocks. She builds them up and knocks them over. Her plastic lamb is boring. She watches her mother run a dishcloth along the windowsill. She watches Linda's familiar back and her bottom and legs, her arm and hand and long hair. She is thinking of nothing, living entirely in the present. A beige blind is halfway up the window with its dangling circular tassel.

Linda, meanwhile, has changed her mind about Port Badminton. She rubs at fly spots on the windowsill, rehearsing to herself the speech she will make to Evan that night.

I can't bear it. I want us to go back to Melbourne.

Evan and Linda had arrived in winter, when the weather was gentle. Now it is summer, and hot beyond belief. Clothes dry within minutes of being hung out on the line. Clothes are wet with sweat within minutes of being put on the body. Linda hates the wet circles under her arms. Her dark hair is sticking to her neck and should be pinned up. She can't be bothered to do it. She can only bear to stand here at the sink with the dishcloth. It's not fair, she repeats to herself. She lets go of all logical thought processes and abandons herself to the mental repetition of some key phrases: *Too hot, Can't bear it, Not fair.*

A small subgroup of Tracker Wives have formed themselves into a Bitching Circle, and Linda is part of it. They have a long list of grievances. Besides the shocking heat, there is no fresh milk, no television, limited radio, nothing in the shops, few opportunities for middle-class children, no

71

culture to speak of, the flies swarm over one's face, sucking at its juices, the mosquitoes eat you alive and give the children nasty red welts and you're forever having to paint them with calamine lotion and tell them not to scratch. One Englishwoman is terrified of snakes and refuses to leave the house. Another wife, stirred into action by her own repeated pronouncements, has already 'up and left'. She has flown back to Perth with the children and is now waiting for a truck to follow with furniture. The husband sends money and all in all finds life more straightforward without her. This sobers the Bitching Circle, turns the volume down. Most of the women just want to complain, not act.

'It's too blinking hot,' blubbers Linda, giving voice this time. She collapses into the kitchen chair, the dishcloth still in her hand. She rubs the damp dishcloth over her arms, enjoying the momentary coolness.

She is tired of the heat, but most of all she is tired of the Bitching Circle itself, the cosy negative web these women have woven for themselves with its predictable gossip and judgements. She has worked hard to fit in to this particular subgroup – the group with the most beautiful furniture and dresses – and now she has done almost too perfect a job; she is right in the centre of weekly tennis and afternoon teas and the company of teeming children. These women are tiring because she feels compelled to perform her Normal or Better Than Normal routine with them. That only makes them want to drop in to talk and smoke for hours. She is widely admired, and her clothes and style are being copied.

And it's too hot.

Linda starts to thump the table with the dishcloth. Jo comes over to hug Linda at the knees. Linda cries harder and louder, patting Jo on the head.

There is a cheerful 'yoo-hoo' chorus at the back door. It is members of the Bitching Circle, just dropping in. When they see that Linda has been crying, their faces form a range of expressions, from concern to embarrassment to poorly concealed pleasure in anticipated gossip ('Poor thing, I think she's had enough').

Linda sits back down at the table, allowing herself to be petted. She throws the dishcloth over the women's heads, aiming for the sink, and grabs a hanky held out to her. It smells of naphthalene. Someone has put lamingtons on the table; someone else has removed the greaseproof paper and is swatting away the flies. The kettle goes on and a tin of Carnation evaporated milk is opened. Linda's closest friend among the tracker wives has an arm around her shoulders but loosens it after a few seconds because it's too hot for bodily contact. The women shoo the children away and lean inwards, waiting to hear.

Linda glances up and sees all their faces, and laughs. She is suddenly laughing at all of them, feeling the laughter bubble up from deep inside her. The more she laughs and fails to explain what she is laughing about ('What's so funny, Linda?' 'Nothing, nothing!') or what she had just been crying about ('Oh, nothing!'), the more she has to keep laughing. She feels them all slipping away from her, feels their bewilderment. She didn't mean to do this, but she can't help it now.

Yes, she can. She pulls herself up with a gulp, stops laughing. 'It's the heat! It's driving me mad!'

Everyone relaxes: a nice, comprehensible problem. Linda is immediately back in her place not just at the centre of the group, but on a pedestal slightly above it. Linda gets them talking about something else. She enjoys her lamington and tea. She feels fundamentally at odds with the aims and values of the Bitching Circle, but for the moment there is nowhere else to go. In any case, there is comfort in a pack, that can't be denied.

The second time Evan stays out to watch for galahs, Linda enjoys the luxury of a whole bed in which to stretch out her long legs. She dreams that she can hear someone calling 'Mrs Johnson! Mrs Johnson!', but it takes some time for her to understand that the voice is calling *her*. She wakes, confused, as the voice grows more urgent. 'Yoo-hoo! Are you there?'

It is Marjorie Kelly from two doors down, enormously pregnant, a green melon about to explode. She is standing beside the EH Holden with her hand on it, as though it is salvation itself, a provider of relief from pain, a transport to a better place.

Linda runs back into the house to bundle up the sleeping Jo, runs out again, throws Jo in the passenger seat, herself in behind the wheel, and starts the engine. Marjorie gets herself into the back seat, her watery eyes not seeing; they are turned inwards, somehow, watching the baby descending into the birth canal.

'I'm sorry to disturb you, Mrs Johnson,' she says. 'Kevin's at sea and I've been waiting for my sister. She's coming soon but I don't think . . . it's not . . . she's not . . . ow!'

'Don't worry about that now,' says Linda. 'You'll be right, we'll be there in a minute.'

The EH Holden is alone on the road, blinking pointlessly at the corners.

'I'm so sorry,' says Marjorie as they pull up outside the hospital. 'I think the baby's here.'

'Don't look,' says Linda to Jo, who is standing on her seat, looking.

Linda leaps from the car and opens the back door to find, by the car's dull interior light, that Marjorie has positioned herself nicely, her nightie all bunched up around her chest, a round head between her legs. Marjorie gives one last push and a baby slithers out into Linda's hands.

'It's a girl,' says Linda.

'Is that a girl?' asks Jo, looking at the slithery thing.

'Thank you, Mrs Johnson,' gasps Marjorie, reaching for it.

'Please call me Linda,' says Linda. She has nowhere to wipe her hands.

'Marj,' says Marj.

Baby Susan, resting on Marjorie's belly, gives a little mew. Linda dashes off into the hospital, holding her hands away from her clothes, shouting. Soon, all manner of people, equipment and a hospital trolley emerge, like ants boiling out of a disturbed nest. Elated, Linda walks down a quiet middle-of-the-night linoleum corridor, searching for a sink.

She finds one with taps with long silver arms meant to be flicked on and off with an elbow.

She drives back to Marjorie's house, where she finds the anxious sister just getting out of her car. Linda is in a generous, expansive mood and wide awake. She tells the sister that everything is in hand.

In the morning Linda washes the back seat of the car using a rag, a cake of yellow soap and a red plastic bucket. The following week, the first of Marjorie's tributes to Linda arrives. It is a crocheted doily distinctly at odds with the modernist style of Linda's home.

FIVE

An affair to remember

AT THE AGE of thirteen, Marjorie won first prize in the Decorated Doll's Pram Parade. She did not push the pram herself; her tiny five-year-old sister pushed it proudly down the dusty wide main road, with the blue first-prize ribbon tied to the pram's handle. But everyone knew it was Marjorie's work. Marjorie stood there on the side of the road with the hatted and gloved townswomen, soaking up the praise.

But this was also the day she discovered that she was plain. 'Plain girls can always cultivate charm,' said a lady from the Red Cross, who was possibly only trying to be kind. Later, Marj's sister confirmed the diagnosis. Marjorie had slumped shoulders; a neck thrust forward at an angle rather than perpendicular to the floor like the girls who mastered the art of walking with books on their heads; and slightly bulgy eyes. No curve at the waist, just a little barrel of a trunk. To her credit, Marjorie was capable of genuine admiration of beautiful girls. She liked to measure them and dress them and make them even more beautiful, without envy.

*

The years went by and the girls she knew all married, one by one. Then the weddings stopped, because they had run their course. She was considered to have been *left on the shelf* when Kevin Kelly unexpectedly asked Marjorie to go to the pictures with him. He stank of whale blubber but she said yes. A girlfriend, on hearing the news, said thoughtfully: 'It doesn't matter what a person is like on the outside, it's what's inside that counts.' She was referring to the stink. All the flensers stank, there was nothing that could be done about it. They could wash themselves for a week and the stench would only fade, not disappear.

On the night of her date, Marjorie's bulgy eyes glittered, her cheeks were pink, her wide froggy mouth was moist and inviting. When she saw Kevin coming down the street towards her he was wearing a boot on one foot and a slipper on the other, and he was limping; the day before, he had slipped in the blubber on the flensing deck and twisted his ankle. Although he'd had four showers that afternoon, he stank of whale blubber and Palmolive soap.

Marjorie's new dress (turquoise with taupe trimmings and accessories) was flattened against her body in the strong wind. She had to use both hands to hold her dress down and hat on. They swept into the Memorial Theatre, dancing on air like movie stars, held up and driven forward by the wind. Kevin forgot all about his ankle. They watched *An Affair to Remember* as the cyclone set in in earnest. 'Keep her going!' the audience yelled when the power cut out and everything plunged into blackness, bringing the sound of the screaming wind into the foreground. Kevin and

Marjorie took advantage of the velvet darkness combined with general commotion to move seamlessly into a series of long kisses. Despite the ominous crashing and breaking sounds, the audience stayed on in the dark for a long time, hoping the film would start up again, unwilling to face the storm outside. Eventually they had to surrender. All had adventures getting home.

After her wedding, Marjorie Kelly moved in to the Kelly place on Clam Street.

It was a well-known house, one of the oldest in Port Badminton. 'Little did I know I'd live in it one day!' she liked to remark.

It was a house full of things: shelves and boxes and corners of them. There were bottles of different-coloured sands, interesting-shaped rocks, bits of driftwood, seashells, and a genuine old Persian carpet. Generations of Kellys had brought things home; things were shifted about but never thrown away. No, you can't throw that away! It might come in handy, or someone might come looking for it. It was Marj's job to live among it as best she could.

When she moved in, the house stood alone on its flood-prone spot at the edge of the samphire flat. Generations of Kellys had been born there; children who liked to hunker in the slightly soggy, slightly salty clay of the samphire flat, studying the succulent bulbs of the reddish, greenish vegetation that grew there. Kevin was the youngest of his siblings. Eventually everyone else died or moved out until it was just Kevin and his mother left in the house. Then Kevin surprised everyone, his mother most of all – *I nearly fell off me chair* – by getting married.

When Marjorie moved in, the old lady was ailing but still shuffling from room to room with the aid of an apple crate that she pushed forward an inch at a time.

'Would you like a cup of tea?' Marjorie would ask. 'Just a small one,' old Mrs Kelly would say, as if to ask for a large one would cause extra bother.

It is a year after Marjorie's first date with Kevin. There is another cyclone coming. In the dead eye of the storm, Marjorie goes outside and stands in the middle of the street with the houses at her back and the low salty scrub in front of her. In the distance, the low scrub gives way to mangroves and, beyond that, unseen, the Indian Ocean and humpback whales. The sky is an eerie navy blue. The world is like a snow dome just after it has been picked up and shaken and left to settle again. It is an uneasy stillness. Marjorie can smell the talcum powder on her sweaty skin. She hears a voice say, 'Hello,' loud and clear. It isn't shouted – the word is spoken at conversational level – but Marjorie knows it comes from far away. Another disembodied voice answers, 'Hello.' Other than that, there is silence. An extreme, vertiginous silence.

Inside the house, Kevin is eyeing off the heavy wooden table in the kitchen. He is thinking that, if necessary, he and Marjorie and his mother can cower under it. Marjorie comes back in, talking about the navy sky and disembodied voices. She finds Kevin under the table. He asks her to join him, to test how comfortable they would be if the roof blew off.

The eye passes and the winds come screaming back in the other direction, trashing Port Badminton thoroughly this time. Two bedraggled men turn up at the mission not far from Chinaman's Pool, shouting over the wind. When the matron opens the screen door, it blows right off.

Banana trees are flattened. Roofs are lifted off houses. Small boats are lifted bodily out of the sea and deposited on land.

Marjorie and Kevin Kelly pass their cyclone in old Mrs Kelly's bedroom, listening to the screaming wind and rain clattering on the iron roof like continuous machine-gun fire. The house stands firm. There is no need to evacuate to the spot under the table. In the morning they celebrate their good fortune, feeling fresh and well.

But then comes the flood.

'She's a big one,' they're saying around town. 'She'll be over the bridge by the morning.'

A hammering at the door wakes them at four in the morning. In the dark, an official from the Shire is telling them that they must leave town right this minute. It's an Evacuation.

Marjorie and Kevin have trouble taking this in. They had already stacked things up off the floor. Their bed linen is on top of the wardrobe; their clothes are sitting in a pile on the kitchen table along with the sewing machine. The bathtub is full of clean drinking water in case the town's water supply fails. Old Mrs Kelly is sitting up in bed, the bedclothes piled all around her so that they will not droop into any water that might lap around the legs. They have matches, candles, tins of baked beans, newspaper for toilet paper and reading, a tiny gas stove with a spare cylinder, powdered milk, sugar and plenty of tea-leaves.

Kevin tells the Shire man to bugger off. Marj murmurs apologetically in the background. But the man refuses to leave. Kevin eventually pushes the man out of the doorway; punches are thrown and Marjorie yells at them to stop.

A policeman materialises out of the night and manages to catch Marj's eye while Kevin is mopping at his bloody nose with a handkerchief.

Marjorie says firmly: 'I'm going with the cop. I'm taking your mother.'

Kevin lets them go, but to save face he insists on staying. The policeman shrugs.

They bundle old Mrs Kelly into the car. Marjorie runs back for her sewing machine. The policeman carries it out for her.

'It's quite heavy,' he says.

'It's a Pinnock,' say Kevin and Marj together.

Kevin passes in the apple crate for his mother. Marj settles it awkwardly over her knees, with the edge pressing into her shins. They drive away.

Kevin returns to his house, the only one he has ever lived in. He sees it with new eyes. He sees that everything is makeshift and worn but comfortable. Marjorie has made a small yellow gingham curtain for a doorless cupboard.

Marjorie and old Mrs Kelly are taken out to the marshalling point at the Forty Mile Tanks on the road heading south. For days, they sit with other families in a camp beside the concrete tanks full of fresh water. The evacuees rig up some shade by hanging grey ex-army blankets between cars. There is much tying on, rolling up, pegging into the ground. They make and eat sardine sandwiches with slightly rancid melted butter and curling stale bread. They wash them down with billy tea and powdered milk and play cards with old scuffed packs. Children run and squabble, enjoying the novelty. Marjorie has brought her knitting. Women notice that she is making little booties and congratulate her.

And then the camp moves on, this time to a temporary town for the people of Port Badminton that has been set up on the cricket oval in Geraldton, a day's drive to the south.

The young mayor, later to be known as Crowbar, stays in town, paddling about in a dinghy, collecting marooned strays, animal and human. Decades later, in his rambling parliamentary speeches, he will declare that his years in Port Badminton were the best of his life. He will begin many a monologue with the words: 'When I was the mayor of Port Badminton . . .'

Crowie arrived in Port Badminton in his early twenties. He got out of his car and looked about him. Here, he could be a big fish: this was clearly a very small pond. Port Badminton, materially languishing somewhere in the 1930s, was overripe for modern improvements.

Crowie built his fortune quickly, gathering enemies, supporters, a bulldozer, employees, contracts, a caravan park, a hotel and the mayoralty. He lobbied government ministers to seal the road all the way from Perth to Port Badminton, arguing that this was a better way to transport bananas than by ship from the One Mile Jetty. Once the road was sealed, he regretted that it brought pests: union officials and other busybodies.

Crowie, accompanied by a stray dog that he has rescued, paddles his dinghy up to the submerged gate of the old Kelly place on Clam Street. He moors his boat by tying it to a fence post and wades into the house through waist-deep water to find Kevin Kelly sitting on top of the old kitchen table. He slides off the table when he sees Crowie and follows him out to the dinghy. As he boards the boat, he and Crowie adopt an exaggeratedly genial tone with each other, calling each other 'mate' twice in every sentence. They both understand the extent of Kevin's humiliation. The dog welcomes him into the tin boat, jumping all over him and scratching him with its long claws. 'Get off me, mutt,' says Kevin, pushing it away.

When Kevin appears at the tent city in Geraldton, Marjorie organises a set of dry clothes, dabs mercurochrome on the scratches made by the dog – they are looking inflamed – and feeds him his first hot meal in a couple of days. But what he really needs now is something Marjorie can't give: a beer. He joins a merry band of men heading off to the pub.

With Kevin drunk for days on end, Marjorie absorbs herself in the activities of the Country Women's Association, slicing polony, making sandwiches, handing them out. She enjoys herself. It reminds her of the war when she was a little girl, helping to knit socks and make bags for parachutes.

As the floodwaters subside, the residents of Port Badminton trickle back into town. Linoleum feels squishy underfoot, meat in fridges is off and stinking, and there's a slick of mud over every surface. Dead fish are found in strange places; for example, wedged in the wire of an aviary, as if they had died trying to join the birds.

Out at the mission, the missionaries notice that the doublegees – sharp, three-horned prickles brought down by the river – are ruining the children's precious shoes. Matron tells the children to save their shoes and wade barefoot through the water on the basis that feet can grow back but soles can't.

A plantation woman notices a little bean plant growing in the silt on the kitchen floor. Her children think this is funny, but she can only think about all the valuable topsoil that has been washed away.

Marjorie, Kevin and old Mrs Kelly return to their sodden home. The sun shines steadily out of a big blue sky, making it hard to believe there were ever clouds and rain and flood.

The whaling station shuts down, and Kevin gets a job on a prawning trawler. He goes out to sea for weeks at a time, returning first to the Port Hotel to drink half of his wages and then, contrite, on to his home in Clam Street. Marjorie shows him the tiny baby asleep in its bassinette.

It is another perfectly formed thing that Marjorie has made in his absence, like a cake or a lady's dress.

To celebrate, Kevin goes out and buys a large tin of paint. He paints his house blue. Just the front, not the sides or the back, because he runs out of paint.

Every year, there is a new baby. All girls.

About a year after John F. Kennedy first announced his intention to send a man to the moon and return him safely to earth, a little team of surveyors could be seen pegging out Clam Street. Along one edge, it was not so clear where the road ended and the samphire flat began. A clearer line would be needed.

Suddenly, the Kellys' humble street is the centre of attention. The Department of Supply has decided not to accommodate the influx of tracking station workers up near the Dish on the red sand dune, but closer to town, to schools and shops for the trackers' families.

As development picked up pace, Crowie stood at the narrow join between the outside world on the one hand and local business and government on the other.

At first, the tracking station was just a small huddle of men in clean white shirts, stark against the red earth, pointing about and referring to notes. Then the large yellow machines arrived to reshape and smooth the dune. Cement footings were poured. Sweat poured down faces and stuck shirts to backs, as men worked in the unbearable heat of the day. They gathered in Crowie's Port Hotel at the end of it to drink ice-cold beer.

When everything was ready, the Dish itself rolled majestically into place. Townspeople, children and barking dogs were there to greet it. It sat on the dune like a giant mushroom, at once casual and purposeful, surrounded by adoring attendants.

And then, all that remained was for someone to press the ON switch.

With the Dish now plainly seen on the horizon, the pace of work in Clam Street took on even greater urgency. Wooden frames went up and shirtless men assembled walls made of wide sheets of Wittenoom asbestos. They cut the pieces to size, unaware of the invisible filaments lodging in their lungs.

In view of the potential for floods, the floors of the new houses were set a few feet up off the ground, unlike the Kellys' place, which had been built straight on the earth. The old Kelly house seemed to shrink and sink down even lower on its haunches as the perky new houses sprang up around it.

As a rejoinder to all this noise and excitement, Kevin Kelly's old mother toppled over her apple crate and could not be revived. She was laid out on the kitchen table for her viewing, but as the weather was warm, she was carted off more quickly than she would have liked.

The sawing and hammering continued regardless. Marjorie Kelly, with small children at foot, watched the progress as she boiled sheets in a copper tub in the back- yard. The sheets, filling with hot air, rose like balloons.

Marjorie had a long smooth stick for pressing them back down into the bubbling soapy water. Her face was pink, a slick of heat and steam.

After her mother-in-law's death, Marjorie made some tactful but purposeful readjustments. The old lady's room was made over as Marj's dedicated sewing room. She installed her Pinnock sewing machine, and nailed a picture of Mother Mary and Baby Jesus on the wall above it. She acquired the wooden dressmaker's dummy, a silent figure to accompany her through the years. The neck, bust, waist and hips were nicely rounded out but the head was a mere stump, a small wooden handle on which someone had drawn a face with a slight smile or perhaps rueful smirk. Two legs were represented by one sturdy pole on a flat base.

She went through the spilling boxes of her mother-in-law's haberdashery, things from before the last war and the one before that, ordering it into jars and tins and small cardboard boxes. She assembled these in the apple crate that the old lady had used as a walking frame, turned on its side to become shelves. She added her own buttons to the Kelly buttons, allowing them to mix in: it was like the blending of DNA.

The children, as they came along, would all be added to one room, crammed into corners and up on bunks. As each new baby graduated from the cot beside the marital bed, Kevin and Marjorie would get to work on the next one. As the children grew, they would guard personal space with lines on the floor marked by floorboards or the edge of a rug. 'Get out of my side!' they would yell, or, when feeling sociable, 'Come over to my side.' And the child, thus invited, would step over the line between old floorboards and feel that she had gone from one room into another.

The Kelly children will not be allowed to set even a fraction of a big toe across the threshold of the sewing room. *You'll smear the fabric with your dirty little hands.* But this will be softened by the promise that one day, when they are old enough, they'll be let in. They will even be taught to sew. But this will not stop the sticky brood. It will be their eternal goal to sneak in, to snatch a look at their mother's sacred, separate territory.

If a child creeps in, Marj will always know, no matter where she is in the house or yard. She'll yell: 'Who's that in the sewing room? Get outta there or you'll get a wallop.'

When she can, Marj will lurk in there, not sewing, just sitting with a cup of tea and a Bex powder, getting away from the lot of them.

As Marj runs down a long seam, she hears a cascade of screeches, human and avian, coming from the front yard. For some time she blocks it from her mind, but the racket becomes so insistent that she lifts her foot from the pedal and listens. She snips the thread, dusts down the front of her dress and opens the front door to have a look. When she appears the noise ceases immediately. Kevin and the tiny girls look up at Marjorie nervously. A child is holding up a bloody finger, a howl on pause. Marj looks more carefully and notices that they are all gathered around a small wooden box with a bird in it.

'Oh, Kev, not a bloomin' galah!' says Marjorie.

There is a general silence. Even the galah seems embarrassed.

'It – bit – me,' hiccups the bitten child.

Kevin turns on his best beseeching/beguiling expression, looking deeply into Marjorie's eyes. She relents, issuing the following orders: 'Take it round the back. Rinse it off and put mercurochrome on it. Wash your filthy face. Set the table. I don't want to hear a peep out of the lot of you. I've got to finish this dress or there'll be what for.'

By the time she'd reached 'set the table' she was back in her sewing room; by the time she got to 'what for' Marj had almost completely trailed off. She was now talking to herself, at work on another long seam.

The new houses in Clam Street sit quietly for a little while, gathering strength. Then the first tracker family moves in, and another. Before long Clam Street has a strip of bluish bitumen down the middle, a footpath down one side and pale, pampered children with neat haircuts riding colourful new tricycles.

Marjorie Kelly is not shy (and has good business instincts). As soon as people move into the street she gives them a day or so to settle before mounting the stairs to the front door with a plate of tarts or lamingtons under a freshly laundered tea towel.

Marjorie taps at a new door. Once inside, she eyes everything off hungrily. She reports her findings to Kevin.

'She's got a kitchen bench with a couple of metal poles sticking up out of it and cupboards coming down off the ceiling. She's already got cafe curtains over the sink.'

Kevin: 'That's quick work.'

Marjorie: 'What's quick, Kev?'

Kevin: 'The cafe curtains.'

Marjorie: 'I'd say she brung them with her.'

Marj copies the cafe curtains, using a remnant of dress fabric.

A sewerage drain is put in to serve the new houses. No more does the nightman quietly arrive from behind, rattling his small flatbed truck to a stop behind the back fence, stealthy as the Easter Bunny. Now, there's the industrious, hygienic sound of water flushing against the new ceramic bowl. While Kevin is at sea, Marj burns the old wooden seat, worn to a shine by countless bottoms, in the fire under the copper. A cement path is made between the back verandah and the revamped toilet. The path continues under the door and into the little room itself. It can now be hosed out easily. A small plastic flower is nailed to the wall. Its hidden plastic compartment houses a crystalline block of a sickly-sweet air freshener.

Everything is ready. All that remains is to add a pink and grey galah in a cage. I am duly installed on the back verandah, facing the outhouse containing the new flushing toilet.

I was a whim of Kevin Kelly's and an extra chore for Marjorie. From my spot on the back verandah, I could smell the waft of scent from the air freshener when someone opened the door. Eventually it lost its smell.

***

Evan Johnson and Kevin Kelly stand in the Kellys' back-yard, each holding a glass of Swan Lager freshly poured from a brown long-necked bottle. Their backs are to the outhouse; they're facing me but not particularly looking at me. Kevin is wearing a blue work singlet and shorts and his feet are bare. His hair is gingery, his eyes as blue as the Indian Ocean and his shoulders are burned and blistered. He has the beginnings of the beer belly that will slowly expand through the rest of his adult life, some years faster than others, like tree rings.

The two men discuss towropes, trailers, diesel generators, roof racks, tarpaulins and eskies.

Linda Johnson and Marjorie Kelly, meanwhile, are standing in Marjorie's sewing room; the dressmaker's dummy is a silent third companion. 'Oh, I can't sew for *nuts*,' says Linda, and she immediately commissions Marjorie to make a sleeveless cotton dress. Within minutes she is standing in her underwear being measured at bust, waist and hips.

Marjorie Kelly's green maternity frock – still worn because it is comfortable, even though she has had the baby – is old-fashioned, voluminous, but clearly well-made. Linda notices the picture of Mary and Baby Jesus on the wall above the sewing machine. Marjorie, in turn, notices Linda's immaculate handbag and slender waist. Each notes these points of difference. At another time and place they might not have been friends but history – in this case mankind's ascent to the moon – has brought them together, and they are glad.

The two women take to sitting on kitchen chairs brought out to the back verandah near my cage. They drink tea – I note how they love tea, and sigh over it – and gossip as they watch the children play. The new baby lies in a bassinette at their feet, surprised by her own arms and legs as they appear in front of her own face. The two women nibble ginger nut biscuits that release a scent I find intoxicating. I poke my open beak through the wire, hoping that someone might put a bit of biscuit in it. They rarely do. If I shriek, they tell me to shut up. From time to time the women intervene in a squabble between toddlers, remove a dangerous object from little hands or disappear inside the house to change a nappy.

Their friendship is mostly carried out privately, just between the two of them. Linda hears all about, but rarely meets, Marj's extended family; the Kellys are not invited to dinner parties with the tracking station crowd, although they do come along for the big all-in barbecue parties held in the Johnsons' backyard, at which smoke billows from a sliced-lengthways forty-four-gallon drum and children run in packs.

When Linda sees Marjorie boiling sheets in a wood-fired copper in the Kelly backyard, the same one slaved over by generations of Kelly women, Linda exclaims over it and magnanimously offers her washing machine. Marjorie is embarrassed and faintly suspicious. She does not believe a washing machine can possibly be as hygienic as a good boiling. On the other hand, Marjorie is so delighted with Linda's friendship that she quells her discomfort and hands over a bundle of sheets and towels.

In those days I was more interested in Jo than Linda, though Jo was barely more than a toddler. She came straight over as soon as she saw me and squatted beside my cage. She examined me curiously. I enjoyed the attention. I fanned out my crest, bobbed on my perch.

'This is what you do,' an older Kelly sister said. She bent down beside Jo, waggled a conductor's finger at me and sang: *Dance, cocky, dance!* Jo followed suit, waggling her finger and singing.

I danced. I even felt the urge to repeat the phrase in my quavering little voice. I couldn't mimic the consonants, but I achieved something approximating the vowel sounds. I easily mastered the rhythm.

Jo was delighted. She scrambled to her feet and danced in front of my cage, a full-bodied dance, her knees bending, her torso twisting. Her white leather sandals had a fringe of leather that flapped slightly with her movements. We danced, looking at each other as we danced. We were two young creatures. Then she sat down again and leaned closer to my cage.

She wanted to pat me. I could tell she wanted me out of the cage and in her lap like a doll. She reached a translucent pink finger into the cage. I was just moving towards it when a bigger hand snatched the little hand away.

'Don't put your finger in the cage! It bites!' She was a bossy girl, that Kelly sister. She shepherded Jo away, in through the back door.

I waited for them to come back out again. The door opened and shut a few times, *thwip, thwip*, but it was always someone else: another little Kelly, or Mrs Johnson, with her long legs, on her way to the toilet.

Jo didn't come back out again that day. She must have left through the front door with her mother.

A few days later, she burst through the back door unexpectedly and made a beeline for my cage. She sat beside me and looked into my pink eye conspiratorially.

'I've pinched a button,' she whispered. She looked about to make sure no-one was watching. Then she uncurled the fingers of her left hand, revealing a small blue button. It had a tiny sparkly stone on top.

'That's a real diamond,' she said. 'Don't tell.' She closed her fingers over it again.

I nodded quickly, briefly opening and closing my crest.

'Where are you, Jo?' came Linda Johnson's voice from inside. And then Marj's voice: 'She loves that cocky, doesn't she?'

But they didn't come out. We were free to socialise.

I pressed my head against the wire and gave a tiny, soft, clicking sound. Slowly, Jo brought her forefinger up to the feathers behind my hidden ear and scratched gently. She knew I needed a scratch even before I knew it myself.

As she hit the right spot, I felt my nictitating eyelids slide up over my smooth pink eyes. Bliss.

Then she ran off again. She was young, like me, but relatively free to move about. I waited for her return. I waited for a long time, returning to my obsessive perch walk, up and down, up and down, through the hours until dark.

Eventually – probably only a day or two later, but time passed so slowly for me then that it may as well have been weeks – Linda and Jo are there again. The tea, the biscuits, the children squabbling.

As the women chat, I listen closely. Linda Johnson brings news of a wider, bigger world. The rich veins of information available to me later – data dumps from the Dish, books from the Book Exchange – are still a long way off. For now I must make do with what comes before my cage; what I can hear in the background; noises that sometimes carry from the street. I try to keep track of information, to work out how one piece might relate to another. I construct mental maps and theories, adjusting them as new evidence becomes available.

The days continue long and hot. And this, Marj tells Linda, is nothing. The heights of summer are yet to be reached.

Back in her own house, Linda notes that the laundry floor is cool under her bare feet. As Jo naps, she takes a book in there, stretching her bare legs over the concrete. Sometimes she takes a spontaneous little nap herself, leaning against the wall, letting her head loll, a little line of drool escaping from the corner of her mouth. She is bored and under-challenged, but at the same time she does not feel moved to spend any more hours than necessary playing tennis or being on various committees (she has so far resisted overtures from the kindergarten committee and the repertory club). She begins to spend more hours in the laundry than she would care to admit. Sometimes her washing machine is silent; sometimes it is industriously grinding through Marjorie's sheets.

***

Kevin Kelly swings off the road to the One Mile Jetty, following a sandy side-track through the scrub to the ruined meatworks where the Dogger lives. He admires the Dogger's Land Rover as he gets out of his own decrepit vehicle.

'Ya there, mate?' he calls, studying the cat pelts hanging from wire stretched from one crumbling concrete wall to another. He waits. After a long interval there is a groan from somewhere inside.

'Time to get up!' yells Kevin to the walls, and listens.

Abandoned before it was even finished, the meatworks was always a ruin. Designed to be an abattoir and packing factory, it failed because the sheep hereabouts were grown for wool, not meat, and the investors hadn't done their homework. It had been – momentarily – an impressive, empty edifice. Townspeople quickly raided it for anything useful: floorboards, copper pipes, glass windows. Now the roofless shell is the Dogger's home. He sews cat pelts together to make soft rugs.

The Dogger appears, filthy and possibly bloodied, although these patches could have been caused by red dirt staining sweat and spilt beer. His shirt is hanging open, revealing scars from a long-ago stoush. He is still a little drunk from the night before.

'You're looking flash,' says Kevin Kelly. 'Why did you go to all the trouble?'

'Do me best,' says the Dogger. He is carrying his rifle. He is ready for action, whatever it may be. He nods courteously, without making eye contact, in the direction of Marjorie and the shadows of little kiddies in Kevin's car. He hops lightly into the Land Rover and starts it up.

The two vehicles set off in convoy in the direction of Shark Bay.

The Dogger drives with his rifle on the seat beside him. He makes appearances before the magistrate from time to time for drinking, swearing and fighting. When these incidents are reported in the local newspaper, they insist on using his given name (William) and he is described as being of No Fixed Address, even though his true address is perfectly well known.

The Dogger is the son of a man who came to Port Badminton to get away from complications that had piled up elsewhere. He lived, angry and penniless, in a shack in the scrub, aided by a woman he'd beaten into submission. One day his own dogs mauled his children. The little girl died but the boy survived, leaving great scars running across his chest and around to his back. The man shot the dogs and a few days later shot himself. The boy and his mother lived on in the shack. He went to school in bare feet and used his father's gun to shoot rabbits for dinner.

The Dogger is practical by necessity but his soul is Tortured and Philosophical. He is not oblivious to the fact that some creatures are lucky and some are not, and that this can change at the drop of a hat. He admires the beauty of low-hanging stars in the night sky and the intelligence in the eye of a mother dingo. He shoots her, but not without regret.

The Dogger enjoyed his first shred of simple good luck when he was nineteen years old and won a government contract to trap and shoot the dingoes. When he told his mother the news she wept for joy over her bottle of Yalumba port. A stroke had left one side of her body limp; not long afterwards she died. 'She died happy,' the Dogger tells himself when he thinks of his mother. He avoids thinking about his father and sister, although they sometimes visit him in nightmares.

The Dogger makes his main living as a dingo trapper but he will also shoot rabbits and kangaroos that can be surrendered for bounty (both are considered pests) or sold for meat straight from his Land Rover in the main street. When it was still open for business, he'd sometimes be called up to work at the whaling station for a few hours, shooting at the sharks that could reduce tethered whales to skeletons within hours.

By dint of evenings spent at the Port Hotel, the Dogger is sometimes drawn into miscellaneous schemes that require the services of a good, straight shooter. The current plan is for a man to waterski from Useless Loop at the bottom end of Shark Bay to Port Badminton at the top, a distance of some ten miles. The scheme has grown under its own momentum as the list of those desiring to be *in on it* expands. The plan is to tow three speedboats by road down to the Loop. Various other vehicles will follow, containing the Dogger, two other shooters, various fishermen and a posse of tracking station men. The main boat will drag the skier, and the other two boats will form a protective flotilla containing a shooter each to pick off any circling sharks. As only one person can be the skier, names are put into a hat. As this is the lucky period of Evan Johnson's life, it was his name drawn from the hat.

The participants head for the Loop. Men and women are nervous, children excited. The wind starts to pick up before they are halfway there.

When they arrive, the children tumble out of the cars and soon discover that the buildings of Shark Bay are made of millions of tiny white angel-wing shells. The shells, compacted together underground over thousands of years, are quarried and used like bricks. The main street is paved with a different shell: pearl shells brought in by the pearling luggers. It's a marine fairyland. The children run down to the water to wait for the dolphins that sometimes come to frolic in the shallows.

The dolphins fail to arrive, so the little tribe of fun-seekers begins to search through the seaweed for worms. If they put the worms in the water, they reason, they may be able to attract the dolphins.

The wind continues to pick up. The seas get heavier. Evan attaches the big wooden waterskis to his feet nonchalantly, but his heart is pounding. Rain begins to squall and drum down on his head as he rises up out of the sea on the end of his rope. He can only see the boat in front of him intermittently between the giant waves. Visibility is particularly poor because his horn-rimmed glasses are back on the beach under Linda's care.

Soon, he is being dragged along underwater. He hears the crack of a gun and loses his grip on the rope. He floats in the water in his yellow life jacket, squinting, thinking about sharks. Then a boat is beside him and he is, mercifully, hauled from the water. 'We're calling it off!' yells the Dogger, rifle in his hand. 'Oh, are you?' says Evan, as if surprised and disappointed.

Within a short time, everyone is in the local pub, discussing the operation. It would have gone off perfectly, they all agree, except for bad luck with the weather.

One day, they'll have another go.

Evan and Linda Johnson drive back to Port Badminton in silence. While the conversation in the pub at Useless Loop was full of bravado, it is impossible to keep it up now that they are alone in the EH Holden, in driving wind and rain, sliding all over the muddy road. They miss a fence post by inches. Linda's right foot involuntarily presses down on an imaginary brake. Evan finds this irritating, but says nothing. Jo sleeps on the blue vinyl seat in the back, sliding around but not waking up.

When they get off the dirt and onto the thin strip of bitumen down the centre of the North West Coastal

Highway, their minds relax away from a united focus on the road ahead and go off in different directions.

Evan's mind goes back to the moment he heard the gunshot and let go of the rope. As he let go of the rope, it was as if he were letting go of life itself. He replays the terror of it. Worse, there is the flavour of premonition about it, a flavour he cannot get out of his mouth. It is as if Time drew back the curtains for just a moment, giving a glimpse of itself, like the moment Gypsy Rose Lee offers a glimpse of her nakedness in a quick flash before the curtains close again. But unlike the glimpse of a naked Natalie Wood, which was very pleasant (was she wearing a body stocking?), this glimpse of naked Time is very nasty. A leering thing. But if he says nothing, if he can just hang on to the steering wheel, this moment will pass, and everything will right itself.

Linda's thoughts, on the other hand, return to the sight of the scars across the Dogger's chest and back as he carried his rifle past the beach towel territory she had made for Jo and herself. She watched him wade out to the waiting speedboat, put his rifle in first, then leap over the side in a light, precise movement.

Evan and Linda are married because Evan, uncharacteristically, did not give the matter careful thought. He is meticulous about his work, undertakes rigorous research before buying an item such as a refrigerator or car, and takes great care of personal items, categorising and labelling them and knowing where they are. He still has the same pencils he had as an eight-year-old, worn and sharpened down almost to nubs. He still has the article from *Hobbies Illustrated* – cut out when he was eleven years old – giving instructions for making a crystal set teapot radio. It didn't occur to him to apply this sort of care to his choice of a wife. He felt himself at a loss in this regard and grateful to Linda for taking the situation in hand. He considers himself very lucky to have a wife so attractive and competent. She cooks and cleans and writes letters on behalf of the family, even the ones to his own parents and siblings. She buys his clothes for him, breaking new socks out of cellophane and adding the old ones to the rag bag, all without discussion. He finds her changing moods, contradictory opinions and propensity for aimless chitchat a mystery, and quite often irritating, but has been reassured by *Reader's Digest* that all of this is normal in the fairer sex.

The marriage of Evan and Linda is like a Venn diagram, two overlapping circles. There's the part in the middle they share, which at first is quite large. This has already begun to narrow down as the two circles move away from each other. Technical information and practical details regarding the Moon Race take up most of the rest of Evan's side of the Venn diagram. He does not share these things with Linda, except in the broadest detail. There are also shadowy memories that can't be spoken about because they are unnamed, like the feeling of being loomed over by an ominous chest of drawers. On Linda's side of the diagram there is a grave sense that she has married the wrong man, or perhaps shouldn't have married at all, or perhaps it would be better to go back to Melbourne and pursue an education, somehow, or visit the Dogger at the meatworks and abandon herself to sexual intercourse on his soft rug of cat fur, or run screaming, naked, up and down Clam Street until she is taken away to a cool, restful sanatorium in the Swiss Alps.

The windscreen wipers swish and smear. Linda allows herself to indulge in the olfactory memory of the Dogger's armpit.

Evan, she notes, seems to have no smell. Even in the heat of Port Badminton, he is a person whose body odour rarely registers. As an animal, he is neutral to other animals. He causes no hackles to rise, no female animals to come running over. He is not sexless. He would appear to be normal sexually. But he has himself no sexual scent, or very little.

At first Linda had no idea that this was a problem. In recent years she has been occupied by Jo, and starting a new life, and then the thrill of getting out of Melbourne and living in a place where the sun bakes off mould and anything damp. But the day came when she was there at the tennis court, waiting her turn, reading the letters page of *The Women's Weekly*. *What can I do?* writes Worried Housewife. *I have no desire to sleep with my husband.* Linda took her eyes from the page, watched the ball go back and forth. Then she took a breath and read the answer: *You must continue to pretend.* Linda read this carefully a few times. Then she casually turned the page, as if the word PRETEND had not been lit up in neon lights. She looked up at Evan, playing tennis like any other husband. He was leaping, arching, delivering a smashing serve. What has this man to do with me? How did I get here?

She looks at other couples. They have a connection with each other that seems bodily, organic, that Linda doesn't feel.

SIX

Bumping around in the shadows

SWEAT IS RUNNING out of Dr Harry Baumgarten's springy black hair and down his forehead. His eyes are keen; he does not need glasses. The author of *The Wonderful World of Australian Insects*, he is on his way to Port Badminton's agricultural research station to study the adult banana weevil. As he drives, he looks out for birds, because he is also a keen amateur ornithologist. In fact, his publisher has asked if he would write a follow-up book to be called *The Wonderful World of Australian Birds*. He is considering this request.

Harry is unusual among Australian men in that he prefers sandals, unlike his peers, who stick to long socks and closed shoes. He likes to air his feet when it's hot, and believes this helps prevent fungal diseases. He drinks espresso coffee made in a little Italian percolator and seeks out controversial or banned books on the premise that if a book is banned, it is probably interesting. A couple of years back, he read Manning Clark's *Meeting Soviet Man* and got into a terrible row at a dinner party after he quoted from it.

While his expertise is in the tiny details – the tiniest secretions of chemical, the tiniest thickness of hair or wing – he also likes to think about the big picture and is not at all afraid of bombast. Where his peers observe social convention in matters of religion, sex and politics – that is, to consider them private, almost like toilet habits – Harry likes to plunge in and draw people out. Sometimes, in doing this, he will come up against a great wall of . . . nothing. He will speak his mind, eloquently and at some length, only to find blankness in the eyes of his companions because they are still thinking, or suspicious, or surprised or offended. What he'd love is a feisty, exploratory, fearless response, but he is in the wrong circles – possibly the wrong continent – for that.

Fortunately, this is offset by his knack for finding something interesting wherever he goes. He might find that the middle-aged wife of a colleague is practising the Japanese tea ceremony, or that there is an unusual variant of moth or meltingly delicious freshly boiled mangrove crabs. He enjoys making small improvements to his systems of work and lifestyle. For example, he has perfected a way of keeping a cabbage fresh and edible for weeks in the desert without refrigeration (wrap it in damp newspaper and keep it in the shade). In other words, he is slightly eccentric, but in ways that don't, on the whole, bother others. He is thus able to slip through the social net of conformity and invigorate his fellow human beings. At a backyard barbecue, for example, he might bring out a bottle with a stick insect in it, attracting the attention of men, women and children alike.

When he is not in the field, Harry lives alone in a flat in Perth, with views of the Swan River. In the lavatory there, he has a framed print of a Picasso nude in which there is something going in or coming out of every orifice. When he has people to dinner he might give them Hungarian goulash with Spanish wine and olives. He is known to have smoked weed and travelled across Europe. When he is in a good mood, he can be thrilling company.

When he arrives in Port Badminton, a frisson goes through the tracker community, to which he naturally gravitates. Wives are keen to invite him to dinner parties. They go hunting for stuffed olives and attach coloured cocktail onions to toothpicks. They're trying to match the standard set by Linda Johnson, who, it is said, hosted a dinner party that was elegant yet relaxed, with conversation both wide-ranging and intimate.

***

The supermarket doors glide apart as we approach. Momentarily, I see Lizzie and me, reflected in the glass. We go down the usual aisles, Lizzie laying in supplies in case we have to stay indoors for a couple of days as the cyclone goes over. Tea-leaves, a tin of evaporated milk, a bag of birdseed, a loaf of white bread, a knob of pale pink sausage called polony. Tomato sauce. It is clear others have been doing the same: the tomato sauce is getting low. The girl at the cash register, in accordance with her training, says brightly, 'How are you today?' Lizzie ignores this but I politely raise and lower my white crest. The girl says, 'Hello, cocky,' and puts the things into two plastic bags. Lizzie hooks her leathery forearms through the handles.

Back out on the footpath, she settles the bags at her feet and organises herself a cigarette.

I think about my reflection in the glass doors. It always surprises me, how small I am. How *birdlike*.

I think about how, all those years ago, Harry Baumgarten hunkered down beside my cage and had a good look at me. It was, perhaps, the only time in my entire captivity that I was seen for what I truly am: a bird. An animal with wings made for flying, a beak made for crushing wild grass seed, a cloaca made for laying eggs. Dr Harry Baumgarten honoured my Avian Self.

We pass the Port Hotel, glance in. There's a big crowd in there, urgent, making sure they have enough liquor or beer or wine to carry them through the storm.

DISH: Stand by. Incoming rueful thoughts Harry Baumgarten.
GALAH: Where is he?
DISH: Anthill country, Northern Territory.

HARRY BAUMGARTEN: It's strange to think that I hardly knew Evan Johnson, the man who – as a thought, a stab of discomfort – would accompany me through the rest of my life. I first saw him at a dinner party at his own house in Port Badminton.

He seemed friendly, contained, straightforward. He

shook hands, offered a beer. He introduced his wife, who waved across the room as she swept a small child off to bed. We ate crackers and drank Emu Bitter as we waited for the others. I was early.

Later, I learned that Evan's father ran a successful hardware shop in Caulfield, Melbourne. His mother played the piano and hosted regular card games. There were five ladies who came to the house, week in, week out, year in, year out. These ladies would burst into gales of laughter, incomprehensible to Evan and his brothers. Evan busied himself over little projects such as the creation of a crystal radio set in an old teapot for his mother. The first time Linda visited the Johnson family home, Evan showed off the teapot. His face in that moment was the face of a child, proud of his achievements.

Linda and Evan met playing tennis. Both considered it time to get married; each saw the other as fitting the bill. (There was probably more to it than this; Linda's account was, by the time I heard it, jaundiced.)

Within a year they had married, moved into a flat and had a baby girl. Linda brought nothing into the marital home but a suitcase of clothes. No small pieces of furniture; no kitchen things, sewing box or trousseau. Evan's mother always made a show of being *puzzled* by Linda. She gave the newlyweds old saucepans and pillowcases from her own cupboards. Evan deliberated over the ideal television set and refrigerator. On the weekends, he made improvements to the flat and helped elderly neighbours carry things upstairs.

Linda was always proud of Evan's mind: sharp and focused; the mind of a mathematician. In another country, another family, he might have been a professor of physics. But as this was Australia, and his family lacked an academic tradition, he had left school at fifteen to become an apprentice radar technician. By the time he met Linda, he was progressing well. Eventually, he supposed, he'd be earning an executive salary. One day, Linda imagined, they'd have a two-storey house with a swimming pool.

But this is not what happened. Flicking through the back pages of the Melbourne *Age*, Linda saw an advertisement for an Experimental Officer Class 3. This officer was required to work at a tracking station on the north coast of Western Australia. The position required experience in 'telemetry, tracking systems &c', but beyond that the description of duties was rather vague. When he read the advertisement himself, Evan understood they were looking for a man with general abilities, someone who could lend himself to whatever needed to be done, electronically speaking. He began to compose his application immediately.

As we drank our Emu Bitter and ate Jatz biscuits, I studied him the way I often studied people I considered to be (unlike myself) 'normal'. Life for Evan Johnson was not a mystery but something to be enjoyed, simply and cleanly, like a game of cricket. I envied this. I wanted it. And yet I didn't want it.

I took a bottle of homemade grappa to that dinner party at the Johnsons'. The bottle had been pressed into my hands by my new Italian friends, the Mastroiannis, who grew bananas and vegetables on the banks of the river. Until then, my existence in Port Badminton had been somewhat lonely and starved. I was sleeping at the Port Hotel and working by day from my base at the agricultural research station. I was gathering insects, studying them under the microscope. I typed my reports on an ancient Underwood.

In my breaks, I read Horne's *Lucky Country* and, for a complete change of pace, dipped into Apollinaire's *Alcools*. I was – have always been – happy in my own company. I would have been quite content to see out my research project in this manner if it were not for the food at the hotel. It was awful: a burnt steak and fried onions, or burnt sausages and fried onions, or burnt lamb chops and fried onions. On a good day, there might be ragged boiled cabbage and a dab of mashed potato on the plate. But worse than the food was the entire lack of it if you missed the narrow window in which it was served. Once the cook had left for the day, the kitchen was closed, and that was that. And there was nowhere else to buy dinner. If it was a weeknight and it was after 5 pm, you were on your own.

So I was grateful when Marco Mastroianni called me away from the base of a banana plant to invite me to a family feast. I accepted the invitation like the starving man that I was. I ate like a wolf, which pleased the womenfolk, and then we spent a vino-soaked evening discussing politics. We all radiated bombast. Everything we saw, everything that someone said, became an excuse for a story or a song. The newborn litter of puppies in the corner led me to mention Rabelais' anticipation of the science of pheromones: he'd found that a smear of the excretion of a bitch on heat could, by itself, attract a horde of male dogs. The Mastroiannis loved this. They talked about hunting for birds, tiny Italian birds, cooking and eating them. There were no more birds in Italy because they'd all been eaten. Not one left? No! Not one bird! Translocated to Australia, they were experimenting with the galah and the little corella. I told them I loved birds.

'As much as insects?'

'*More* than insects.'

I was only allowed to leave by promising to come back soon. As I left, we shook our fists. Down with Imperialismo! Up with Socialismo!

The hotel cook discovered my infidelity. He seemed to want me back.

'I could extend the dinner hour,' he said, catching me one day before I went out. 'If you're going to be working late.'

But I no longer needed him. For the first time in my life, I was being lionised. The Italians had loosened me up, given me social confidence. One dinner invitation led to another and another; as a single man living in temporary accommodation I was never expected to reciprocate. It was a very good lurk. I was free to reinvent myself. I could shed the bookish caterpillar and become the dashing butterfly. Thank you, *la famiglia* Mastroianni.

I had stored the bottle of grappa in the bottom drawer of the rickety wardrobe in my hotel room. I took it, now, to the Johnsons to offer as a digestif. But as the story of its provenance – homemade in a makeshift still by Italians on the riverbank – sparked immediate interest, we drank it first as an aperitif, and then through dinner as a table wine, and afterwards with dessert. It was pure rocket fuel.

Drunkenness was instant and thorough. The conversation slid to Linda's feathered carrots. A tracker wife held one up and said, 'For heaven's sake, Linda! How long did it take to do *this*?' We looked again at the platter in the centre of the table and saw it with new eyes: the carefully arranged tendrils of celery curling back on themselves; the radishes opening out like little accordions; the wafer-thin, leaf-shaped pieces of carrot notched down the sides to suggest feathers. Their effect stood somewhere between the poignant and the ridiculous. An attack of giggles overtook the table.

Then the conversation swung from hilarity to intimacy. We began to tell our earliest memories, our greatest fears, our deepest secrets. Or ostensibly so. I noticed that people – me included – dredged up fears and secrets that were entertaining but not too close to home. Then it was Linda's turn.

'My father is a communist,' she said. 'My mother lost her entire family in the war and she's quite mad.'

This was serious stuff, a tonal shift. There was a moment of silence. I looked at Linda tenderly. I saw that she was a kindred spirit: an outsider overcompensating, in this case by feathering her carrots. And now, because of my grappa, she was about to spoil the image of conformity she had worked so hard to achieve.

I egged her on.

'Was your family ostracised?'

She paused, sizing up the spirit of the hive. She knew with Donald Horne, that *in the narrow shaft of clear bright sunlight of the Australian mind, there was little room for the idea that we might all be bumping around in the shadows*. She was willing to step out of the sunlight.

'Yes,' said Linda evenly. 'I was called names at school. Commo. Reffo.'

Then, trying to tell us about a girl with psoriasis sitting alone on the school bench, she burst into tears. She was crying because she had left that poor girl behind when she got her own invitation to play a stupid skipping game. She had not looked back.

And then the others, emboldened to step out of their own narrow shafts of clear bright sunlight, offered shadowy stumblings of their own.

'School can be such a nasty, nasty place,' said a tracker wife with feeling. 'Children can be very cruel. I was called fat.'

Our eyes could not help but lower themselves to her plump midriff.

The confessions continued. Evan Johnson told us he had cried in front of the whole class after being whipped with a cane.

'Were you ostracised?' shouted the plump tracker wife.

'Yes!' we all cried in unison.

No-one wanted the night to end. Someone suggested a drive out to the One Mile Jetty. Evan and Linda looked at each other and murmured the name of their sleeping daughter.

'You go,' said Evan. 'I need to get up early in the morning.'

We piled into two cars. Linda drove my black Zephyr. She had admired it, so I passed her the keys. I sat beside her; a tracker couple sat in the back, nursing my guitar.

'I like the way you toss back your hair,' the plump wife told Linda. 'I think you have panache.'

'Lots of panache in that hair,' I said, picking up a hank of it and letting it drop.

We walked out on the One Mile Jetty, listening to the waves slapping at the pylons. I slung the strap of my guitar around my neck and provided the occasional strummed accompaniment to our raucous discussions. We went all the way out to the end, where there was an old storage shed, all locked up now. We sat down with our backs against it, looking at the moon and its refracted reflections in the water. We were trackers and scientists. The moon belonged to us.

A fish leaped out of the water, its silver flank catching the moonlight. We sang the following moon-related songs:

Moon River

That's Amore

and

By the Light of the Silvery Moon.

The next morning, of course, I felt like hell. I wondered who he was, this new Harry Baumgarten. What on earth was he up to? Did I like him? The thin notes of the chiming wedgebill penetrated my skull: *Did ya get drunk? Did ya get drunk?*

'Yes, indeed I did,' I replied.

At the Johnsons' dinner party I'd expressed an interest in going out to visit one of the twin islands that lay just off the coast. Linda offered to help: one of the Johnsons' neighbours worked on a prawning trawler that would soon be departing.

And so it was that I was able to roam over a small uninhabited island, enjoying the solitude, seeking out birds, taking notes in a small leather-bound notebook with a short stub of a pencil sharpened occasionally with a penknife. I set up a microphone in a bit of wind-swept scrub, learning how to use my new recording equipment. Wind was a problem, so I spent time experimenting with windbreaks and fashioning windsocks.

I gathered driftwood and gnarled grey twigs to make a fire on the beach. I ate sardine sandwiches on stale bread. I swung my billy through the air three times, arm completely outstretched. As I did so, I imagined looking down on myself, a tiny figure:

A man
alone on a small island in the Indian Ocean
swings his right arm around like a windmill
observed by seagulls.

I was thinking of Apollinaire:

Tranquil bird
lower your second eyelid

I wanted to consult my copy of *Alcools* but I hadn't been able to find it for days. Where was it?

At dusk, I was bitten by sandflies; maddened by them. After dinner, I sat on a dune and looked out over the sea at welling lines of luminous phosphorescence.

DISH: Over.
GALAH: Is that it? Anything more?
DISH: Ants.
GALAH: Hold the ants. Roger.

'Yes, big cyclone, Lucky!' says Lizzie. 'Let's get you home, snug as a bug in a rug.'

Emergency vehicles are cruising the streets with loud-hailers. We're being told to GO INSIDE. Lizzie does not pick up speed. We head for home in our usual languorous manner, hair and feathers ruffled by the wind.

***

'That entomologist is also interested in birds,' says Linda to Marjorie the morning after the dinner party. 'He'd love to go out and look at the seabirds on the islands. Do you think he could go out on Kevin's boat?'

Linda wants to impress Harry, and Marj wants to impress Linda. Kevin is ambushed by these desires as soon as he gets home that evening.

Marjorie says: 'That insect man is also interested in birds. He wants to go out to the islands on your boat. Do you think you could line it up?'

Kevin doesn't like lining things up.

'What does he want to go out to the islands for?'

'To look at the birds.'

'What does he want to look at birds for?'

'To study them.'

'I thought he was an insect man.'

'He is, but he also studies birds.'

'What does he want to study birds for?'

'I don't know – he records them, he's got a tape recorder.'

'One of them reel-to-reel what's-its-names, is it?'

'How would I know? You'll see it if he goes out on the boat.'

Thus enticed, Kevin lines it up with his boss and the big day duly arrives.

Harry arrives at the Kellys with an army surplus backpack slung over one shoulder. He waits for Kevin near my cage, having a cigarette, tapping ashes discreetly into an old cooking pot planted out with nasturtiums. I have an opportunity to study Harry Baumgarten from head to toe. Unexpectedly, he does the same in return.

Harry Baumgarten looks deeply into my pink eyes, then casts his own brown eyes over my rosy breast. I flush and turn my face to one side and raise my pale white-pink crest so that he can see it to best advantage. I fan out a long wing, showing the deep colour of the underside. He keeps looking at me steadily, so that I feel undressed by him, de-feathered. He can see all the way down to the contours of my naked skin, to the touching thinness of my neck. He sees my airy, lightweight bones, made for flying. He does not attempt to make me dance or sing. Afterwards, he stands slowly, throwing me a last appreciative glance.

Kevin Kelly appears, winding a long piece of rope, looping from elbow to hand, elbow to hand. I am feeling strangely peaceful, whole. I have been *seen*.

*

Harry is soon on the deck of the trawler, enjoying the open sea.

Kevin and the other deckhands are working around the boat; Harry is observing, taking a keen interest, asking a lot of questions. No-one minds. In fact, the crew is more than happy to have him. Kevin is proud of his connection to Harry, the pest man and birdwatcher, or entomologist and ornithologist, if you want to use the correct lingo, which Kevin does, after practising a couple of times in his head. The men show Harry over the boat, watching him take it all in. Eventually, they assemble down in the hold, around Harry's khaki army surplus backpack. Harry carefully unwraps his new microphone and Tesla tape recorder. He names the birds he is aiming for.

The crew nods as if they, too, were interested in birds.

Kevin asks Harry how much he paid for the recording equipment, and whistles softly when Harry tells him.

Everyone gazes at the things on the table, enjoying the expensive sight of them. One of the crew would like to set it all going, sing a couple of songs, have them played back. He imagines everyone gathered around the microphone singing 'Swing Low, Sweet Chariot' in four-part harmony, but he doesn't have the confidence to suggest it. He watches regretfully as Harry carefully puts everything away.

Then Harry, feeling on top of the world, gets the things out again, and says, 'Let's record ourselves for posterity! This marvellous moment, upon this marvellous boat, on this marvellous day! Which one of you gentlemen would like to go first?'

Buoyed by this enthusiasm, the crew member steps forward to the mic. He sings, low and beautiful, *Swing low, sweet chariot*, just as he imagined he would.

He sings the whole song, all the verses, with the entomologist singing harmonies.

The others watch and listen, rapt. As soon the last note sounds, Kevin prances over to the mic with a song he sometimes sings in the shower. It's about an Indian brave and his sweetheart facing each other over a raging river. Kevin knows a fair bit of it by heart. All the men, stone cold sober as they are, join in the chorus:

Running Bear loved Little White Dove
With a love as big as the sky
Running Bear loved Little White Dove
With a love that couldn't die!

Actually, the singing never occurred. It flashed through the minds of the crew members as they looked at Harry's recording equipment. They watched him pack it away again, and said nothing.

They approach the first island at Hospital Point, skimming over darting fish.

'I've heard that these islands were prison hospitals for Aborigines,' says Harry Baumgarten. 'One island for men, one for women.'

'It was some sort of leper colony,' Kevin confirms. He would like to offer more information but he knows no more about it than that. Then he remembers something he'd heard as a boy. 'Some tried to escape but they were eaten by sharks.'

Harry hops out of the dinghy in thigh-deep water, holding his pack and sandals over his head, and makes his way onto dry land. He stands on the shore, his wet shorts clinging to his thighs, watching as the fishing boat motors away. The crew watches Harry as he recedes into the distance. Another boat, coming through in the opposite direction, will pick him up in two days' time. Once Harry is off the boat, they miss him, although none would mention this.

Linda leaves Jo at Marjorie's house and drives away, luxuriating in a personal autonomy she has not known for years. She is twenty-four years old and free; as free as a married woman can be in a small town with watchful eyes. She has a purse with a bit of money in it – not much, it is true – and a car with petrol in it. For an hour or two, she can go anywhere she likes.

She decides to go for a solo drive to Pelican Point. She drives over the causeway and down the dirt track, knowing this will be noticed, knowing someone will say, 'Oh, I saw you yesterday, you were going out along the causeway,' and there will be a pause while that person waits for an explanation, not because they are suspicious, necessarily, but because they are just chatting and this is something to chat about. Linda stops the car on the hard ground behind the dune that serves as a car park for beachgoers and sits there for a minute, replaying scenes from the dinner party. She gets out and takes herself for a midweek walk along the beach. There is nobody else about, except for a large pelican.

On the way home she stops off at Quan Sing's haber-dashery and mercery opposite the war memorial and buys a couple of yards of printed cotton fabric. After dinner, Linda mentions to Evan that she bought some fabric for a new dress and also went for a little walk on the beach. Evan registers this information with as much interest as if she'd said, 'Today I mopped the laundry floor.'

The next day, in town and among her friends and acquaintances, nobody remarks that they saw the Johnsons' EH Holden heading out over the causeway. Clearly, she has done nothing remarkable or unusual.

She did, however, take Harry Baumgarten's *Alcools* with her to Pelican Point. The pelican saw her reading it.

Tranquil bird with inverted flight bird
Who nests in the air
At the limit where our planet shines
Lower your second eyelid earth dazzles you
When you raise your head

She'd seen the book on the passenger seat of Harry's Zephyr as she took the driver's seat. At the end of the night, after waving everyone off and returning to the silent kitchen – a bombsite of dirty dishes – she found she had it in her hand.

A few days later Evan flies out to the Goddard space centre near Washington, D.C., for a three-month training course, leaving Linda with the EH Holden and a freewheeling entomologist.

***

Cyclone Steve's advance party is here. It's still not certain whether he intends to doss down in town or just wave from a distance. Either way, they're battening down the hatches in the caravan parks, shouting at each other to move it this way and that. Fishing boats are heading prudently back to shore.

Tropical Cyclone Steve, a male cyclone with a beer belly and long, grey, windswept hair, thongs flapping at his feet, formed out of the ether somewhere in the Pacific. He spun like a dervish, gathering force from water and wind. He first moved in towards the Queensland coast to biff at coastal towns, leaving them flooded and dishevelled. Then he moved north, pummelling the coast as he went, not out of rage but out of sheer high spirits, blissfully unaware of damage, inconvenience and insurance premiums. On he went, up over the two points at the top of the continent, before his joyous slide down the western side. Now he is finally starting to tire. He is almost ready to cross the coast and call it a day, becoming, as they say at the weather bureau, a rain-bearing depression.

But he's still dangerous, no question about that.

The Dish is hauled into lock position, its aerial pointing at a perpendicular angle to the ground, its bowl turned perfectly upwards, like a teacup held level. This is a more stable position against cyclonic winds.

Kevin Kelly, a volunteer with the One Mile Jetty Preservation Association, is at the wheel of a tiny faux steam engine. Once a week, he is rostered on to spend the morning taking tourists for a run out to the end of the jetty and back. He waits for his passengers to settle before beginning his introductory patter. This lot will be the last ahead of the cyclone. He shouldn't even be taking these, but they'd looked at him imploringly. They had only meant to duck in to Port Badminton for some groceries and a quick look around town before heading off to see the dolphins, but now they've been told the roads are closed in both directions. They'll be stuck here for days in their hired motorhome. Kevin had relented.

Kevin explains how a little steam engine used to drag bales of wool to waiting ships. 'This one runs on diesel,' he adds quickly, in case anyone is stupid enough to ask (it has happened).

The wool, says Kevin Kelly, came in from the giant sheep stations on camel teams driven by turban-wearing Afghans. The word 'turban' escapes him. He points at his own terry-towelling hat to convey the idea.

The camels used to drag their laden wagons down the main street and turn into Dromedary Lane. 'What does dromedary mean?' he asks the children suddenly.

They look at his red face blankly.

He tells them: 'Dromedary is a fancy word for camel.'

Mid-sentence, he stops to catch his breath. His face has gone purplish against his faded hat; his cheeks and nose are a riot of broken capillaries. There is an anxious silence. It was always a *thrill* when a ship came in, he gasps. Kevin starts the motor, and resumes talking normally. 'Ladies loved it. They got their dress patterns and whatnot.'

As they clatter away from the shore, the passengers glimpse muddy sand and seaweed between the big gaps in the old grey boards, and then swelling green water. They pass fishermen walking in, hunched against the wind, their plastic buckets beside them.

Kevin's passengers disembark. He tells them to be quick, on account of the weather. They get out and look at the choppy water. Seagulls cry against grey clouds on the move. Without being told, they almost immediately return to their little seats.

After the tourists have gone, Kevin potters about in the kiosk, closing things down. There's a stand of wire frames holding postcards: *Port Badminton – The Sun's Winter Home* and *I Fished The One-Mile*. A laminated poster urges visitors to contribute to the Jetty Preservation Fund because the jetty is rotting away and, without an injection of funds for maintenance, its future is in doubt. The fund is housed in a catering-sized instant coffee tin with a slot in the lid. It is full of ten- and twenty-cent coins contributed by penny-pinching grey nomads: no match for the slapping waves.

Kevin's anger has risen steadily, a little more every year, like the layers of fat around his middle. He feels it at his temples, in the arteries of his neck. Not long ago his heart imploded and Marj had to call an ambulance. He had an operation that has bought him some extra years.

But what to do with them?

Marj doles out pills for him and makes matters worse by banning the remaining pleasures in his life: beer, cigarettes, and those large yellow things called rock cakes, a kind of cross between a scone and a biscuit, studded through with bits of burnt sultana and eaten with a good slathering of butter. For years, Kevin bought these cakes from the True Blue takeaway shop where he also bought his Winnie Blue cigarettes and a can of Coke. The girl used to get these things ready as soon as she saw his car, so that by the time he got inside she'd have them lined up on the counter, her hand hovering over the till. It was a pleasant ritual. But now it's the end of all that.

Marj says, 'Why not try a diet lemonade?'

Kevin Kelly says nothing. He is ropable.

Kevin is thinking about a woman who is not his wife. She is at least twenty years younger than he is. He holds an image of her in his mind: her summer frocks, her red hair, her strange, wide-set cat's eyes. Her name is Kimberly.

Marjorie Kelly grabs a kitchen chair and carries it out to the cracked cement path between the back of the house and the toilet. She leaves the chair in that position for a moment as she goes back inside the house, reappearing with a large brown ceramic ashtray in her hands. She hoists herself up onto the chair. The chair, with its spindly chrome legs and old foam seat, rocks unsteadily. Shifting her weight to compensate for wobbliness – surfing – Marjorie looks down at heavy object in her hands. It still smells faintly of thirty years' worth of cigarette ash despite the fact that she has scrubbed it clean with hot water and dish detergent and set it to dry on the windowsill. After Kevin's heart attack, she had wrapped it in layers of newspaper and tucked it into a dark corner of what the Kellys have always called the Long Cupboard.

Then she'd had a thought. Why was she even keeping this ashtray? Smoking was unhealthy. Nobody should smoke. If they did, they'd have to do it right out in the backyard, behind the toilet. So there was no need for an ashtray.

It's difficult for her to do what she is about to do. The Kelly house has always taken things in, given them a home, found a spot. It rarely destroys or throws away. But she has decided to follow through. She holds the ashtray above her head. She'd bought it because she thought Linda Johnson would be impressed by it. Linda had not even noticed it.

She lets it fall from her fingers. It dashes itself satisfyingly against the cement, spraying tiny pieces all around. Nimbly, she climbs off the chair. She picks up the large jagged pieces and wraps them in the expert manner of a butcher or fishmonger, the way her mother had taught her to wrap scraps. She gets out the dustpan and brush and sweeps up the tiny bits.

There. It's gone. Kevin need never know.

***

The houses in Clam Street were for married trackers; the single men's quarters were less salubrious. A long, functional building was made for them opposite the seawall; they slept in four-to-a-room dormitories. It was like boarding school without a housemaster, cook or laundress. The single men had to work things out for themselves. One brought with him a grey cat – he liked to say it was a Russian Blue – called Samantha. Samantha travelled to Port Badminton by road in a sturdy cardboard box, hissing and wailing at first, then giving up the ghost. *I'm dying. See what you've done.*

Installed in her new home, she quickly commanded the respect of the single men by lashing out with tooth and claw if asked to move from a comfortable chair. She would return later, to those with whom she had fought, and expect to be scratched under the chin. At night, she moved freely from bed to bed, forcing grown men to curl uncomfortably around her. They went fishing for her, bringing back tasty whiting to be fried in butter and served to her on a platter.

As Samantha's second birthday drew near, the single men decided that it should be celebrated in style.

News of Samantha's party travelled quickly through the tracker community. Babysitters were booked. Hair was done. On the evening of the party, Samantha greeted the first few wellwishers and then, annoyed at the din, stalked off into the night.

Linda leaves Jo with Marjorie and goes along to the party by herself. She can do this, she tells herself, because she has *panache* and because she needs to return *Alcools*. She won't stay for long.

As the party intensifies, it does not escape notice that Linda Johnson is spending a disproportionate amount of time talking to Harry Baumgarten. She is seen passing him a book, and he is seen exclaiming warmly and going to put it safely in his leather satchel. He returns to Linda after that, and they continue their animated conversation.

There is hilarity all around them, but they pay no attention. Someone falls backwards into a wall, cracking the Department of Supply's new pale green-painted asbestos sheeting. Someone else stumbles about calling, 'Samantha? Where are you, Samantha?'

Harry says to Linda: 'Tell me, what did you see in Evan? He's a good man, but don't you find him dull? A woman like you must find him a little dull.'

For this part of the conversation they have moved to the laundry of the single men's quarters. Linda sits balanced on the edge of the concrete laundry tub, her feet resting on a kitchen chair. She is drinking vodka from a silver cup. Harry leans against the wall nearby, a long-necked bottle of beer in hand. He scratches at an itchy spot left by the biting sandflies out on the island. He lifts his shirt to show a stomach aflame with red dots and scratch marks. 'They're all over me,' he says. 'On my back, down my legs. They itch like hell.'

'Let me have a look,' says Linda.

Harry puts his beer bottle down carefully on the floor of the laundry, under the concrete tub, out of harm's way. He steadies Linda as she gets down from the tub.

From across the yard, a couple of trackers notice them entering the single men's sleeping quarters. They exchange glances.

Linda and Harry are a little unsteady on their feet. Samantha is on one of the beds, a leg over her shoulder, licking. She stops, jumps off the bed and scoots out the door. Harry removes his shirt entirely so that Linda can see the extent of his spots. Linda laughs and says they are very sweet. She reaches out a hand to touch them. Someone opens the door.

'I think I may be allergic to sandflies,' Harry tells the tracker who appears in the doorway. 'Darned itchy.'

'Calamine lotion,' says the tracker, entering the room. 'My kiddies were going mad with mozzie bites until we painted them in the stuff. Calmed everything right down.'

Harry begins to scratch himself, recklessly. He scratches his stomach and tries to scratch his own back. Linda and the tracker move forward to help. The three of them work together on finding the right places and scratching pressures.

'Oh my *God*!' says Harry. 'This is such bliss. Don't stop.'

But eventually they do stop.

Harry is overtaken by a desire for calamine lotion. He thinks about this lotion – thick and pink and calming – in his tent. He has been camping out at Ticklebelly Flats, preparing to record the chiming wedgebill.

'I think I'll be getting off,' he says. 'Hooroo.'

He wants to keep scratching himself in private. Nothing else matters.

After three or four hours of sleep, Linda wakes up, thinking about the party and the scene in the dorm. She senses that there would be something not quite right, biologically or emotionally (leaving aside morally or socially), about an affair with Harry Baumgarten. When he took his shirt off, showing the red dots against the whiteness of his skin, he seemed more a brother than a lover. Their pheromones had little to say to each other.

It is an understanding that Linda shoves to one side. She loves him, she loves to talk to him, and the thought of spending the rest of her life with Evan Johnson is suddenly untenable. She must act now. She thinks of Apollonaire's giddying words:

And they flew.

She decides to go and talk to Harry this minute. She gets out of bed – Jo is still safely asleep at Marjorie's house – and puts her party dress back on, smoothing it down. She splashes her face with water and goes back out to the EH Holden.

As she settles into the driver's seat she feels that the car is watching her, sadly, thinking of Evan far away on the outskirts of Washington, D.C., learning about the rendez-vous and docking of two vehicles in earth orbit. But she starts the engine just the same, and drives off to find Harry.

Did the practical, unemotional Evan Johnson experience jealousy when he saw his wife and Harry Baumgarten together? When, under Harry's influence, she announced to the assembled dinner-party guests that she was the daughter of a communist, did Evan notice and flinch? If so, it would have been hard to pick. He was looking forward to his training course at Goddard; he was immersed in the Gemini mission, the bridge between Mercury and Apollo. He was writing lists and packing bags and checking things. He was polishing his horn-rimmed glasses and sharpening his pencils. Perhaps he was jealous, but perhaps more than that, he simply trusted Linda to use the EH Holden for wholesome purposes only.

*****

I envy those without jealousy and fear. I feel mine rising with the wind, threatening to overwhelm me. I know Lizzie wants to get back to *The Lore of the Lyrebird*, to read it secretly when she thinks I'm asleep.

Despite the homeliness and sentimentality of our relationship, I think she wants to get rid of me. She thinks I'm too clingy. I know she doesn't like the way I drive off visitors, her grandniece in particular, the one who has been to uni and has a nice car and works out on the islands restoring habitat for threatened species. She'll stand out in the yard calling, 'Aunty! Aunty!' until Lizzie goes out to her. They'll talk for a long time. Recently I think I once heard the grandniece say: 'I don't know, Aunty Lizzie. She bites people and poops everywhere. She's high maintenance.' What was that about?

Sometimes she will cart Lizzie off to hospital for check-ups.

'You stay here and be the guard galah,' Lizzie will say. 'Won't be long.'

She'll shut the back door, pulling it to with a click.

I'll be left alone for hours, simmering in my own stew. Lizzie is probably *lingering*, lapping up time away from me, being with her relatives. She might even be having a take-away coffee with the grandniece, sitting companionably on a bench on the seawall, looking out over the water. Just thinking about this makes me go weak with jealousy.

**

Evan Johnson, blue biro over his heart, is thinking about his wife and the entomologist. He sees them together, so neatly matched, like brother and sister. He puts this thought in another part of his mind – seals it off the way Linda might burp and seal a Tupperware bowl before putting it in the fridge – and focuses on the calculations, their comforting scratchings across the blackboard.

'Incoming private thoughts Aunty Lizzie,' says the Dish.

'No,' I say. I don't want to know. I'm right here on Lizzie's shoulder. Her thoughts are right there, on the other side of hair and skull.

'But it's –'

'No, not authorised, delete, go away,' I say.

'I think it's important,' says the Dish.

'NO!' I screech, in English.

'Shhhhh,' murmurs Lizzie soothingly. 'I know you don't like the cyclone. We'll be all right.'

The Dish is behaving strangely. It never used to *argue*.

SEVEN

True Blue

KEVIN AND MARJORIE Kelly sit on old kitchen chairs on the back verandah. They are attempting a moment of *innocent happiness* – so simply and easily achieved in the past; more difficult now.

The wind is rising and rain seems imminent but, sheltered on three sides, they feel quite cosy. A tendril of smoke from a green mosquito coil rises up into the fading light. Kevin watches the end of the coil, which has a soft grey burnt end, a long one, that has not yet dropped away. The little metal holder looks like a tree trunk; the green coil itself like the branches and leaves of a flat round tree.

Kevin brings his glass to his lips. He is drinking diet lemonade. He can taste the chemicals in the fizziness exploding on his tongue. He watches as the burnt end of the coil falls lightly, soundlessly, to the plate, revealing the glowing red tip.

By 10 pm, the air is at maximum humidity, almost dripping. Kevin and Marjorie lift themselves up out of their chairs and prepare to go to bed.

Marj says: 'I'm just going to mow the lawn – I mean clean me teeth.' Especially when she is tired, Marj is liable to mix up phrases with rhythmic similarity. Or she'll come to the middle of a sentence and find nothing there, no more words.

She says, 'I'm just going to put the –'

She says 'what's-it' a lot, or 'what's-its-name': 'Put it on the what's-its-name, Kev.'

He knows what she means. He puts the plate with the spent mosquito coils on the kitchen sink, ready to be cleaned up properly tomorrow.

They take turns making the short trip along the cracking cement path to the toilet.

One at a time, they swish through the bead curtain hanging between the kitchen and the hall. The beads, of amber-coloured hard plastic, clink softly together as they have through the decades.

A pair of tea chests serves as bedside tables. Inside the chests, originally brought to Port Badminton on a ship that docked off the One Mile Jetty a lifetime ago, there are rarely used blankets and never-used wedding presents and a shoebox of mysterious photographs and postcards bequeathed by an unmarried uncle and some of the children's first drawings and toys. Every ten years or so, a returning child will ransack one of the boxes, strewing long-lost items all over the bed, sucking greedily at memories. Marjorie has topped each tea chest with finely crocheted cotton doilies.

They lie under a thin white sheet. Even this thread-bare sheet feels hot on the skin. A small fan whirrs on the dressing table, slowly looking from right to left and back again, through the hours. Kevin and Marjorie Kelly lie side by side, habitually fighting the tendency, caused by their sagging mattress, to roll in towards each other. They move in and out of sleep in the wet air, sometimes waking at the same time, sometimes listening to the fan or the other person breathing or gently snoring.

Marj's voice suddenly pipes up, fully awake.

'Do you want the radio on, Kev?'

'No, it's all right, love.'

'I don't mind, Kev. If you want to hear about the cyclone.'

'No, it's all right. Let's get some sleep.'

Marjorie sleeps, but now Kevin is wide awake. He looks at the ceiling, thinking about Kimberly's red hair and fresh summer frocks, the sun touching her bare shoulders. He is writing her a letter. He adds a sentence here, a sentence there, when Marj is not looking. At first, the idea of a letter startled him. Then he found himself composing it in his head. And then, he was actually writing it.

With Marjorie snoring gently, Kevin Kelly gets out of bed, goes to the Long Cupboard and retrieves the small lined writing pad he has been using. His blue biro is still on the table with yesterday's *West Australian*.

The writing pad has been in the house for at least thirty years. On the front of the writing pad is a photograph of a young woman in a bikini sitting on a sweep of white sandy beach, smiling at the camera. Other swimsuited people are dotted along the beach in the distance. Palm trees stretch out over the sand, yearning for the blue ocean like pot plants stretching towards window light. When Marj brought the pad home thirty years before, she had left it on the table after she had put all the other groceries away. As the afternoon wore on, everyone had given the cover a bit of a glance, Kevin and all five children. They had noted the girl's excellent figure, especially Kevin, who had experienced a tiny peak of sexual interest. But now he does not give the young woman the slightest glance, does not wonder how old she'd be now if she were still alive. Instead, he lifts the cover and looks at his own handwriting.

Dear Kimberly.

He wants a cigarette. The other eight letters of his life were all written with the help of cigarettes. He makes himself a decaffeinated instant coffee with skim milk and no sugar.

The wind is strong outside. Their sinewy ginger tomcat is curled up on Marjorie's chair, his abdomen rising and falling slightly. With his pen in his hand, Kevin looks at the cat but thinks about Kimberly. Her colouring, come to think of it, is similar to that of the cat. She has freckles across her upper arms and darker more concentrated ones on her forearms. She isn't young, but she has kept a marvellously flat stomach. She has straight white teeth and sometimes laughs loudly.

She used to own a fish-and-chip shop in northern Queensland. She emptied plastic bags of frozen chips and battered fish into wire baskets, lowering these into boiling vats of oil. She chatted to her customers, wiping the benches with a hot soapy dishcloth, raising the wire baskets to reveal the golden food. Salt, vinegar, newspaper. Her customers liked her.

When she was a little girl, she went on a talent show on TV. She sang 'Feed the Birds' from *Mary Poppins*. Now that she's a member of parliament, she's on TV all the time. *Keep Asians Out*, she says. A reporter asks her whether she is xenophobic. She has never heard this word before. She says: *Please explain.* Kevin pays attention, liking her boldness, her refusal to apologise for herself.

As he touches pen to paper the colour in his face rises, redder and redder. He feels like a schoolboy writing to a girl he likes, not a citizen of Australia writing to a politician.

Dear Kimberly,

Don't take any notice of what they say about you people are so afraid to say what they really think but your not. Good on you! I am sick of politicians lieing cheating stealing just to get there lifetime superannuation. But you are standing up for the ordinary person, the AUSSIE BATTLER.

YOUR not scared to ask the curly questions!

Look at the Abo's getting handouts left, right and centre. Look at them, driving around town in their new cars. They don't even look after them. They run them into the ground and then they get another one. Where does all the money come from? The TAXPAYER! You and me. Something's wrong with this picture.

Kevin is pleased with this sentence. He repeats it to himself, his lips moving ever so slightly. Something is wrong with this picture! Kevin's mind forms a vague picture of the ideal Port Badminton, with offending elements erased from it.

There is the generous wide street, and there are all the people he has known up and down it, women in frocks, men in hats, children clean and orderly, all greeting each other in a friendly way, standing on the footpath talking, like people used to do. One or two Aborigines are there, dressed as stockmen, possibly even riding their horses, the red dust clinging to their clothes. There are no Aborigines filling up big cars at the service station. There are no big cars, only honest to goodness dust-coated Land Rovers complete with dangling canvas waterbags.

Kevin Kelly has made speeches at his daughters' weddings, warm and funny once he got going, and better the fifth time than the first time, but never any other sort of speech. Now, he imagines himself up before a crowd of people at the Civic Centre, glancing down at his notes – this very page – every now and then, warming to his theme, and getting applause. Standing back, licking his lips, taking a sip from his glass of water. Kevin toys with the idea of offering himself as a candidate. He might even suggest it in this very letter. He sits back in his chair, deep in thought. Why not give it a go? Then he imagines a television crew advancing towards him, the fluffy end of a boom microphone stretched out towards his mouth, and the wind goes out of his sails.

Outside, the wind is beginning to howl and moan.

Kevin gently puts the pen on the table. He gazes at his cold, half-drunk cup of decaffeinated coffee. He looks at the sun cancers and liver spots on the back of his hand. Weak; weak and old. Kevin Kelly may be angry about Aborigines in big cars but he is just as angry with Time. It has tricked him, failed to give adequate warning that one day it would be like this. *Please explain: what has this hand to do with me?*

Hey, True Blue, Kevin whisper-sings to himself. *Don't say you've gone. Say you've gone out for a smoko, and you won't be very long.* He is crying for himself, for his life, his own soul, the one separate from Marjorie and the kids.

Kimberly. Kevin writes, slowly, using just her first name, then a full stop. There is something intimate about this tiny full stop.

Kimberly. Your a very attractive woman.

Kevin's pen comes to a halt, frozen on the page, stuck to that last full stop. Where did that come from? Now the letter is ruined. He can't possibly send it.

Kevin looks up in the direction of the door, expecting Marjorie to appear there, scolding or shaking her head in disappointment and dismay. But no-one is there.

Kimberly, do you know who you look like? You look just like Deborah Kerr in An Affair to Remember. *The same red hair, the same graceful style. Did you ever see that film? An 'Oldie but a Goodie'.*

Kevin is back in the swing now.

They weren't spring chickens, Cary Grant and Deborah Kerr. And nor are we. But —

Treacherously, Kevin allows himself to contrast Marjorie, his wife, with Kimberly Lamb, the breath of fresh air in Australian politics. He thinks of shapeless Marjorie in her shirts and slacks, and shapely Kimberly in her sleeve-less summer frocks. She's always in a new outfit, just like Deborah Kerr on the ocean liner in *An Affair to Remember*.

She must have had a really big suitcase for all those clothes. You never saw the suitcase.

Kevin is now writing a secret love letter. He has decided to finish it and send it anonymously. He'll sign it: *An Admirer – Political AND Personal.* He'll have to find an envelope, buy a stamp. How much is a stamp these days? He has lost track.

His heart is pounding. This isn't good for his heart. He picks up his pen.

I like your sundresses.

Marjorie used to wear sundresses. They were dresses with straps over the shoulders, with her bra straps held in place by little loops fastened down with press studs. Marjorie hasn't worn such a dress for a long, long time. Sometimes, in the bedroom, she will lift an arm and shake the hanging flesh and say: 'Look at me flabby arms, Kev.'

Kevin puts his pen down and thinks about Kimberly Lamb in a sundress, a sprinkle of freckles across her décolletage. Kevin knows this word, décolletage. Living with Marjorie for over forty years, with the paraphernalia and jargon of the dressmaker, has given him special insight into this female realm. He and Marjorie are interested in each other's work. Marjorie will expand on the lovely décolletage of a client and the bit of lace showing above the cleavage, and Kevin will listen, and then he will talk about holes in prawning nets, and she will listen. He has watched Marjorie haul things around, her skinny brown legs, her barrel-like body strong, quite masculine. She could have held her own on a prawning boat if she'd had to. So he knows about this word, décolletage. And below the décolletage. Under the sundress, nothing except a slip of a bra and panties. Her shapely figure. Her waistline. Kevin is breathing harder, looking at the words he has already written, no longer reading the meaning of them. He picks up his pen.

We could go out to a restaurant and dance the night away.

Kevin imagines himself out on a date with Kimberly. They are not spring chickens but they're still in the prime of life. These events are taking place in a city, possibly New York. He is standing on the top floor of the Empire State Building and she's running through the city to meet him, but this time she'll look where she's going, not get hit by a car, and she'll meet him, slightly breathless, on the top floor with views all around. They'll have dinner in the revolving restaurant – is there a revolving restaurant on the top of the Empire State Building? – looking down like carefree gods over the glittering city. With glasses of wine. What wine should he choose? He would rather have a beer, but romance dictates wine. Then he has an idea. He could say to the waiter, 'What would you recommend?' That's it. And then he imagines looking over at Kimberly. She smiles slowly and says, 'Wouldn't you rather have a beer? I know I would.' That's the kind of woman she is, marvels Kevin. A down-to-earth woman, but with grace and style. When the waiter comes, he'll look him straight in the eye and order two beers.

Your my kind of woman, writes Kevin.

EIGHT
Cyclone Steve

THE DISH, IN lock position, is now communicating directly with the residents of heaven. It finds a signal from Evan Johnson and they talk shop, just like old times: blocks and runnels of figures and coordinates pour back and forth in perfectly straight lines through whipping clouds and driving rain.

The wind is screaming now, and it is time for our threnody. With all the breath we can muster, Lizzie and I join each other in our death wail. Lizzie's keening blends with the wind; mine is not quite so harmonious. In fact, mine is rather staccato – my windpipe was not made for the long, drawn-out vowels that Lizzie can manage: Aaaaahhhhhhhhhhhhhh . . . oooooooo . . . aaaaaahhhhh

We shriek: *Get FUCKED. Get FUCKED. Fucken, fucken FUCK!*

We do this under cover of the noise of the cyclone. Nobody can hear us. Or if they can, they must know that during cyclones, normal social bonds are loosed. If an old woman and a galah wish to shriek their way through it, then that is all right.

To work herself up to the threnody, Lizzie tells the story of the teacup and the chains and the islands. She needn't say all of it; shorthand will do.

Camel train – jetty – island – sharks. It's the story that lives inside my teacup; if you drink from it, you can see glimpses of it, in full colour.

Her mother was taken by camel team from her home in the interior, all the way to Port Badminton on the coast. She was a criminal: her crime was to be the possible carrier of venereal disease. The punishment was isolation on the islands off the coast of Port Badminton. One island was set aside for men, the other for women.

For the journey through the scrub, there was a wagon for male prisoners, a wagon for female prisoners and one for two government officials in long socks, sturdy boots and pith helmets. And there were drivers, guards and dogs. Little writing desks were loaded and unloaded in the evenings so that the Longsocks might write reports. The polished legs of their desks sat in the red dust. Before retiring at night, they'd chain up their prisoners and dogs and say their prayers. They were engaged in a bit of *practical detail* relating to the preservation of health and hygiene in the state of Western Australia. They'd unlock all the chains in the mornings, but prisoners were forbidden to leave the moving wagons. Some died on the way, causing delays.

To keep their spirits up, the prisoners shouted to one another from wagon to wagon. The male camels came on heat, foaming thickly at the lips. Bits of thick foam, the consistency of stiffly whipped egg white, would fly off and hit you, if you weren't careful. This was something to watch for and laugh about. And there was a rhythm to the moving wagon, good for napping and dreaming.

And then the land came to an end, lapped at by a body of glittering water stretching to the horizon. The prisoners were marched out along the One Mile Jetty, glimpsing the sucking water in the gaps between the planks. A stinking pearl lugger was waiting for them – the stink was from the meat still clinging to the shells. It took the prisoners to the twin islands separated by a deep, fast channel.

Lizzie's mother carried with her, all the way, a dainty teacup with a broken handle. It was a present from her days as a kitchen maid in a pastoralist's kitchen. Every time she thought she'd lost it, she found it again.

When Lizzie's mother was assigned her stretcher in the long hospital tent, she lay down, eagerly waiting to die. She listened to the flapping of the tents, the roar of the ocean. She thought about her home, her boyfriend on the other island and her old job in the kitchen, where she could eat bits of cake and jam.

Eventually, she began to feel hungry, and this drove her from her sickbed.

Once off her stretcher, and feeling surprisingly well, there was nothing else for it but to join the strange life of the women's lock hospital. Even on a small island consisting of nothing but canvas tents, there was a lot of work to do. Laundering sheets, cooking dinners, patching and mending. In their free time, they were allowed to go out and catch small animals, and cook them over a fire. Lizzie's mother was not happy, but she got used to it. A nurse taught her to read and write using whatever scraps of reading matter might be found. They laboured over the sentences, each word requiring new explanations, new story-ways.

Probably one of the greatest evils of tight-lacing lies in the fact that healthful breathing is thereby rendered an impossibility.

Cyclones would hit without warning, turning everything topsy-turvy, sending things scudding into the sea. Then everything must be set up again, lashed down with sturdier rope.

After ten years, the government sent out a letter – On Her Majesty's Service – announcing that the twin lock hospitals were to be closed. The prisoners were dropped off on the mainland, left to fend for themselves. Lizzie's mother had nothing but the clothes she wore, and a dainty teacup with a broken handle. She stood on the jetty with her fellow prisoners, uncertain about how to proceed.

The teacup, as it turned out, was her passport to new employment. Hearing of an influx of trained servants, a doctor's wife had arrived early to choose the best. The one with the teacup caught her eye.

Lizzie's mother thus returned to domestic service. But she was haunted by the lock hospital and how she got there, and the people who had died on the way, and the government dogs that had snarled at her and all the men who had casually made use of her.

If she had a bit of time off, she'd wait on the main street for the camel teams to come in. She'd study the red dirt clinging to their fuzzy sides. She'd touch it, to touch a little of the country of her birth.

One day, there was a great roaring sound. Children screamed and dogs barked as they ran along beside a machine driven not by horses or camels but by some mysterious energy within. It was a motorised truck, piled high with bales of wool. After that, more trucks appeared, and fewer camels.

A destitute cameleer takes the pins from his camels' noses. He chases them, screaming at them, until they run in all directions, some into the desert, some down the main street of Port Badminton, where they are arrested for causing a nuisance. He stands in the middle of Dromedary Lane and curses Port Badminton, wholeheartedly, fulsomely. He says:

You are a donkey
A monkey
A prostitute town
Fuck your trucks
You have no moustache
No manhood
I spit on your mother's grave
I shove my leg up your arse
May you suffer
And all your children and their children
May they suffer a thousand torments
And curse the day they were born.

Passers-by watch the entertainment appreciatively, not understanding a word.

Lizzie's mother was taken into the doctor's house, and into the doctor's study, in which there was a comfortable day bed for reading and for conducting sexual intercourse with housemaids. She quietly bore the doctor's children, continuing to sweep and polish his house through each pregnancy.

Lizzie's mother and her children lived in a shack on land that would one day become the yacht club. Lizzie was the youngest, and shy. She preferred animals to people, and birds most of all. Her mother, using the pedagogical technique learned during her years on the island, taught her to read and write using scraps of newspaper and magazines.

Gold-fish are very delicate, and you have injured them, we fancy.

The wooden seawall was built, and all the doctor's children, black and white, liked to play on it, to run along its narrow, single-planked top. They also understood, without ever being told, that the official and unofficial children must regard each other as belonging to separate worlds. The official children might suck on boiled lollies; the unofficial children might often go hungry. They all knew each other's names, of course, and played together surreptitiously.

When she reached her teens, Lizzie began work at the hospital, mopping floors and scrubbing out toilets and basins. She had a habit of stealth, of imagining herself invisible. She loved to read the newspaper and have a cigarette in her breaks, but rarely joined the conversations that swirled around the corridors and back rooms of the hospital.

Lizzie was well into middle age when she met the Old Patient. She had been mopping the floor, pushing the mop head right under his bed, when she stopped to listen to a flock of little corellas flying overhead. They listened together. He said: 'Beautiful, aren't they?' And Lizzie, instead of pretending she hadn't heard, said simply: 'Yes.' They continued their discussions in tiny increments over the days and weeks that followed. A mention of the weather, a query about morning tea. He was a rich old pastoralist whose wife was dead; his fortune was being circled by avaricious children. He was taking much longer than expected to die.

Lizzie would linger in his room fractionally longer than necessary, to discuss lambs, or lambing, or the price of wool: she knew about these things because she was interested in sheep, and in her breaks she had been reading the newspaper from one end to the other, including Livestock and Shipping.

The Old Patient got well enough to be discharged to his town house in Oyster Street. He asked Lizzie to move in to help care for him.

Lizzie said yes, before she thought about it too much. She liked him.

Was she his girlfriend, a boarder, a maid? It was never quite clear. But they were very comfortable together. She still ironed her uniform and went off to hospital each day, but now she ran home during her lunch break to make sure the Old Patient hadn't fallen out of bed or cracked his head on the tiles in the bathroom.

He paid for an aviary for the backyard and they filled it with budgerigars, cockatiels and finches. It was more work for Lizzie, but she loved it. This was her calling. She began breeding birds and selling them on. She became a little more sociable, because she had to, for the sake of the aviary and the Old Patient.

I see the Old Patient and Lizzie sitting in their backyard on two old wooden chairs. On a tea chest between them there is an aluminium teapot, a Vegemite jar full of white sugar, a tin of Carnation evaporated milk with two holes punched in the top, a teaspoon and an old strainer. They drink from chipped enamel mugs. A wall of aviary birds is cheeping.

They are comfortable in the shade under the wide canvas awning. They speak only of what is before them, and then only briefly, to save the Old Patient's throat. They breathe only this moment's air. When they fall silent, it is in contemplation of the cracked concrete beneath their feet or the articles of clothing on the clothesline.

Sometimes the Old Patient thinks about the death of lambs, white skeletons in red earth. He remembers the bliss of a scalding cup of tea when work was done. That was the best tea. He says, laboriously, putting his hand to his throat: 'Is this the same tea we had before, or a different one?'

Liz replies: 'It's a different one. Do you like it?'

The Old Patient nods.

The aviary birds cheep and twitter all day, doing all the talking.

When the Old Patient finally stops breathing, Lizzie begins her death wail. Alerted by the eerie noise, neighbours appear, and then an ambulance, and then church ladies begin to take matters in hand, disappearing into their cars with bundles of the Old Patient's clothes to be redistributed at the mission. The avaricious relatives arrive on the scene.

But the Old Patient's will is perfectly clear: they can have the farm, but Lizzie will have the house in town.

At the declining Port Badminton Club, where elderly gentlemen woolgrowers still take a few drinks in their best town clothes, they shake their heads in wonder. *He gave it to an Abo?* The old bugger was clearly being contrary, like the rich New York ladies who leave their fortunes to their poodles.

After the death of the Old Patient, Lizzie retires from the hospital. She likes to walk slowly about town. Eventually, she appears with a galah on her shoulder. She is nonchalant about it, acting as if it has always been there. She is welcomed warmly at the Port Badminton Book Exchange. At home, she reads and listens to the radio and tends her aviary and cleans up after her galah.

Like me, Lizzie has been lucky. Whether by chance or choice, she has made a series of deft moves. Her sister's children were stolen and given to white families to raise; Lizzie, who had no children, was spared this. She had no home of her own, but found someone to give her one. Her relations would like to move in, but she has a ferocious, jealous galah – that's me – to drive them away. She works in her aviary and takes long, leisurely walks about town.

The wind is still howling, but Lizzie is spent. As she gets older, her cyclone threnodies get shorter.

'That's enough,' she says. She kisses me and goes to bed.

What was the nature of Lizzie's relationship with the Old Patient? Was it mere cupboard love – love of the one who feeds and waters you – or was there more to it than that?

And what about my own love for Lizzie? Is mere cupboard love at the bottom of it? Is cupboard love such a bad thing, if it is the only thing available?

Linda Johnson, on her way out to see Harry Baumgarten, was pursuing a *pure* love, not love tainted by the cupboard. A reckless, extreme sort of love that would go anywhere it needed to go. To hell with propriety, security and other middle-class preoccupations.

'*And they flew*,' she whispered to herself at the wheel of the EH Holden.

I'm jealous of Linda Johnson, long gone from town, no longer the driver of an EH Holden. I'm jealous of her long legs, her human form, her ability to impress and even possibly mate with the magnificent entomologist, Dr Harry Baumgarten. I feel my own short legs – not even legs – my squat shape, the impossibility. He *saw* me, he *saw* Linda. But Linda is of his own kind, and I am not.

Still as the wind howls, I can imagine myself as Linda, at the wheel of the car, my foot on the accelerator, enjoying the delicious, delirious moment of possibility. On all sides, as the dawn breaks, the chiming wedgebills strike up a chorus:

Did ya get drunk?

Is pure, human–avian love possible?

Ambrose Pratt tells the true story of James the lyrebird and his relationship with a Mrs Wilkinson who lived in the Dandenong Ranges in Victoria in the 1930s.

Although happily married, James, looking for something more, befriends a plump, cardiganed middle-aged widow who lives alone in a beautiful house surrounded by wide verandahs. James adores her, and to show his adoration, he dances and sings for her. His performances are breathtaking, a marvel to all who witness them. His tail feathers curve over his body, forming a fringe over his eyes as he faces his audience. His dance steps are light and supple. His original compositions freely reference all the sounds he has ever heard, from a dog barking to a tree being sawed to the songs of other birds. During the mating season each year, quivering with passion for his own lyrebird wife – who watches ardently – he returns to his own innate song, the song of himself. This is a simpler song, but utterly haunting. Afterwards, he moults. He loses his magnificent feathers, hiding them carefully as they fall off, and during this time he prefers not to be seen by Mrs Wilkinson. He withdraws from society, using this time to grow a new set of feathers and perfect new songs. Suddenly, he will reappear with a new repertoire, more elaborate dance steps, more complex melodies and rhythms.

James has never been caught or caged or locked up. His love holds not a trace of cupboard love, because he is not offered food in exchange for his performances. They are freely given.

Mrs Wilkinson is humbled by James's beauty and artistry. She knows it might be best to simply receive what is given, lightly and non-possessively, but she can't help her desire to show him off. This is how James came to be known by Ambrose Pratt, President of the Royal Zoological Society of Victoria, and how he became the subject of a collectable hardcover book, a slim but elegant volume with its own photographic plates and the silhouette of a lyrebird on the front, embossed in silver.

Mr Pratt and the other guests arrive by motor car and take their places on the verandah, where they are served refreshments. Sooner than they dared hope, James himself quietly materialises. He stands in the dappled light not too far away, as the assembled audience quiets itself to a reverent silence. Then, all eyes expectantly upon him, James begins to preen his long feathers, carefully and thoroughly. This takes twenty minutes, giving his audience adequate time to examine his beauty.

Then he takes a step backwards and opens his beak to a magnificent overture. According to Ambrose Pratt, his concert pays tribute to the following birds:

(1) The magpie.

(2) A young magpie being fed by parent-bird.

(3) The whip-bird.

(4) The bell-bird.

(5) The complete laughing-song of a kukuburra.

(6) Two kukuburras laughing in unison.

(7) The black cockatoo.

(8) The gang-gang.

(09) The rosella.

(10) The butcher-bird.

(11) The wattle bird.

(12) The harmonious thrush.

(13) The scrub wren.

(14) The pardalote.

(15) The thornbill.

(16) The starling.

(17) The yellow robin.

(18) The golden whistler.

(19) A flock of parrots whistling in flight.

(20) The crimson rosella.

Afterwards, when James has melted back into the bush, the audience agrees that he has also incorporated the sound of a rock-crusher at work, a hydraulic ram and the tooting of motor horns.

Unnoticed by the audience on the verandah, a variety of small birds had also attended the concert, taking up position on nearby branches. They were every bit as enthralled as Mrs Wilkinson's invited guests. In the silence after James's final note, a pair of harmonious thrushes looked at each other in wonder. His version of their song was both loving tribute and a distillation of its essence, better than anything they could have sung themselves.

Can I even call myself a bird? Can one so reliant on supermarket food, books and television really be a called a bird? You may feel moved to reassure me that I had no choice but to abandon my birdness. That the hand of fate overwhelmed personal choices. But there have been times – quite a few times – when I might have flown. After a few weeks with Lizzie, I was fit and healthy and still young. I felt the energy surging through my shoulders at the base of my wings. The long feathers of my clipped wing had grown back. I knew that, physiologically, I could do it. Or at least *try*.

But just at that moment, Lizzie called me to the table for a cup of tea. I turned my back on the blue sky. I guzzled my tea. I danced on the table as Lizzie stirred her mug. I nibbled a biscuit. Lizzie laughed and kissed me on the beak. Afterwards, we napped, companionably, and the call of the wheeling flock receded from my mind.

I have never flown, or mated, or laid an egg. My right wing is clipped. Yes: Lizzie, too, clipped my wing. I am a lopped, waddling, pet galah.

NINE

Chinaman's Pool

It is dawn and Linda Johnson is driving into the scrub looking for Harry Baumgarten. It is the morning after the wild party at the single men's quarters and she's pretty sure she can find his camping spot.

'I'll be catching the morning chorus at Ticklebelly Flats,' he'd said.

She pulls up near his khaki canvas tent, noting in the smudgy early light the remains of his neat fire and the blackened billy. A tea towel is pegged to a guy rope. She gets out of the car slowly, conscious of her long dark hair, her long legs. She can almost hear *swelling music.*

His face appears out of the flap of the canvas tent. His expression is comically quizzical, like a man in a silent movie: *Now who might this be?* She is preparing to smile becomingly when he disappears abruptly back into his tent, without a word. Linda leans on the car, arms folded, looking at the tent containing the body of the man she loves. He emerges a moment later, fully clothed, with a pair of binoculars slung around his neck.

'Good morning,' she says, seeing that it is hopeless, but holding on to a tiny sliver of hope.

His reply is to take hold of his binoculars, as if he is about to hold them up to his eyes and look off into the distance. The air smells fresh.

'Good Lord,' he says. 'This certainly is an early visit.'

Linda sags back against the EH Holden. Tears spring into her eyes.

Now that he has got his words started, they come thick and fast. 'I've decided to start with the chiming wedgebill. They're a dime a dozen, so it should be a breeze. I've got a twenty-foot cable. I'm going to tie the microphone to a likely shrub and then back off and sit quietly. I'm sure it'll be quite splendid.'

'Which one's the chiming wedgebill?' asks Linda dutifully, as if she is his niece on a camping trip.

'That's the "did ya get drunk?",' the friendly uncle says. He whistles the tune. In reply, a real one pipes up.

The shit bird. *Birdus shittus*. Others join in, their calls cycling round and round, taunting her. *Did ya get drunk? Did ya get drunk?*

'Would you like a cup of tea?' asks the friendly amateur ornithologist.

'No, it's all right,' says Linda. 'I think I should be getting back. I just came out for an early-morning walk.'

Linda turns and gets back into the car, slamming the door more loudly than she'd intended, desperate to get away as quickly as possible.

As she drives off, she glances back at him in the rear-vision mirror, standing there with his mouth open as if frozen in a game of statues.

Linda is driving back down the highway. Every minute, there's more light in the day. The colours of Port Badminton are coming to life out of the greyness. The red of the earth. The grey-green of the scrub. The dusty grey line of bitumen down the middle of the road. A gently strengthening blue sky. A brown and white dog is trotting loosely beside the road, perfectly at ease. It's time for Linda to go home and boil up a pot of tea and hope that no-one has noticed her car's unusual movements. It's time to put herself to bed for a couple of hours before going to retrieve Jo, saying a few inconsequential words to Marjorie about the party. She is bound to have a dreadful hangover but there can be a long shower, another nap in the afternoon, another dip into the book she's reading. Everything will be all right if she can simply identify the next appropriate action and carry it out.

But Linda is driving like a wild thing, her accelerator foot flat on the floor. Tears are streaming down her face and more are welling up in her eyes, blurring her vision. She holds the steering wheel with one hand and belts at it with the other, as if boxing its ears. The brown and white dog recoils from the veering car. Linda stops, lights a cigarette and draws back. She winds the window down and breathes smoke out into the air. Calming down.

She gets out of the car and goes to sit under a big old tree, the trunk smooth from many other bottoms. The water at

Chinaman's Pool is perfectly flat and reflective, like a mirror. She stubs out her cigarette and lights up another one and continues to sit. She says aloud, 'Oh, bugger it,' and belts the tree trunk with her left hand.

The Dogger, sleeping in the long grass behind the Port Badminton Hotel, is woken by these words. He opens his eyes, with some effort because the lids are stuck together. He moves his head slowly from side to side, getting the blood moving. He turns onto his side and rests his head on his hand. There in the middle distance, on the bank of Chinaman's Pool, a beautiful woman with long dark hair is undressing. She is unzipping her dress, removing her underwear, shaking off her sandals. Moving silently, the hunter reaches for his rifle. He brings the rifle to his shoulder, training the crosshairs on Linda's back, buttocks and legs as she lowers herself into the water. He can hardly believe his luck.

She swims two wide circles and returns to the bank. She climbs out of the water, the Dogger's sight moving from breasts to belly to the triangle of dark hair. She dresses quickly and then sits down on the smooth trunk to buckle her sandals.

Then she gets up and throws a stone into the water. She watches the concentric circles until the biggest one reaches the riverbank. She'll go home now.

'Can you make it skip?' There's a disembodied male voice coming out of the bush, a friendly voice with a little laugh in it. A barefoot man has materialised. His clothes are caked in red dust. He has the beginnings of a black eye and a cut on his forehead and a streak of dried blood across it.

'No,' says Linda. 'Can you?'

They know each other, but they've never spoken personally.

'Nah.'

They both laugh. She doesn't mind that he has been watching her. He's in worse shape than she is.

'How was your evening?' she asks, looking at his face.

'It didn't go too well,' he says, feeling at his eye and forehead with his fingers. 'How was yours?'

'Not much chop. I drank too much and did something silly. Were you in a fight?'

'Musta been,' he says. 'Were you?' And they both laugh.

'Oh, don't make me laugh,' he says. 'It hurts.'

Linda looks at him openly. He stands there allowing himself to be looked at. Galahs watch with interest from the trees.

'Can I bother you for a ciggie?' he asks.

She lights one for him and passes it over. She sits on the tree trunk as he smokes, saying nothing. Their pheromones mingle in the air between them, getting to know each other.

'I'd better get going,' she says.

But she doesn't move.

Their pheromones are dancing the mazurka.

He sits down next to her on the smooth trunk. His hangover is dissipating like magic. He is careful to sit close but not actually touch. They sit quietly side by side for a long time – perhaps as long as thirty seconds – before she turns to him, noting that he is filthy, blood-caked and reeking of alcohol. Without further hesitation, they dive into the sweet water of opportunity.

Before she even turns the corner into Clam Street, wild galahs have carried the latest gossip all over town.

Linda goes to pick up Jo. Jo is sitting in Marj's washing basket with two small Kellys, pretending it's a boat. She holds out her arms when she sees Linda, just as she did yesterday. Kevin Kelly is there, sitting at the kitchen table in a white singlet. There may be a slight leer on his face – or is she imagining it?

When she gets home, things are in the same places on the kitchen bench, in the bathroom, in the laundry. Everything is just going along as usual, inviting her to do the same.

Linda swears off the entomologist and the Dogger and all men who are not her husband. She cleans the house with great vigour.

But just as the galahs tuned the Dish, the Dogger's phero-mones have tuned Linda's body. She is like a radar, now, sweeping the vicinity, hoping for answering blips from a dirty Land Rover. She imagines him driving out into the red-earth country, over stones, among wildflowers, a radius of hundreds of miles. He sets his traps and comes back to shoot the dingoes neatly between the eyes.

From the top floor of the old meatworks, through the crum-bling open rectangle that was once a well-made window, he sees her sliding down the back of the sand dune. She is walking this way in her tennis shoes and slacks, casually, turning her head to scan the horizon. The coast is clear. It's a hot, windless day, but it's never silent. There's always the hum and thrum of life. There are insects teeming both above ground and below it. Lizards scuttle out of the way; ants are crushed under the pressure of Linda's shoes. The cat fur rug is soft against her bare back.

Linda and Jo run into Harry at the supermarket. Linda is very smooth. She stops and wants to chat, even though it would seem that Harry would like to get away. She detains him in the aisle, asks him about his research, what he is reading. She even asks if he is still troubled by insect bites. Her early-morning visit to his tent has been airbrushed from history.

Jo sinks to the floor to study the bottles of turpentine and methylated spirits on the bottom shelf.

Harry tells Linda he has gathered all the data he can about the adult banana weevil and he'll be leaving shortly, going back to Perth, where he'll write a paper. He has also decided to accept his publisher's invitation to write *The Wonderful World of Australian Birds*. He doesn't mention the chiming wedgebill.

Linda is interested in all of this. She imagines herself writing a paper; she hears the satisfying ding of the typewriter, feels the weight of the carriage return under her hand. She will miss Harry and his attention to her mind. Nobody else cares about her mind.

'Well, hooroo, then,' he says.

'Bye,' she says, bending down to set Jo on her feet.

The Dogger is driving along the red dirt track, expertly avoiding sand traps that could keep him bogged for days. He has a load of scalps in the back, and pelts, and whole dead kangaroos in a pile. He would like to make a little extra money, make some new small improvements to his home, now that it sometimes – this is still astonishing – plays host to Linda Johnson.

He is making good progress when the temperature gauge suddenly begins to climb from C to H. His fanbelt has snapped.

In among his tools and necessaries, there's an empty red cardboard box. Printed on the flap is a sentence that he has paid no attention to until now. DETACH END FLAP AS A REMINDER TO REORDER.

He is in trouble. The vehicle will not get far without a fanbelt. He is in the middle of nowhere with little food and water. There's nobody – with the possible exception of Linda, but this is by no means guaranteed – to miss him. It might be weeks before the Shire wonders why the Dogger is taking so long to deposit his scalps. His concerns shift rapidly down the hierarchy of human needs from sexual satisfaction to the requirements for basic survival.

He does, however, have a pile of moist kangaroo bodies and a knife. He could eat them down, suck their blood. But this is not what he has in mind. The skin of a kangaroo is, after all, a type of leather. Fanbelts for Land Rovers are normally made of cord and rubber, but they *could* be made of leather.

He sets to work in the hot sun, skinning and making strips. His hands and arms are covered in kangaroo blood; it soaks into his shirt, smears his trousers.

He fashions a series of fanbelts. He knows the raw leather will stretch immediately and have to be replaced, frequently. He gives it a burl. It works.

The Dogger finally coaxes his vehicle into town.

He heads straight to the Port Hotel for food and icy beer.

On his way, he sees a group of workmen standing beside a truck. One nods to him. The workman is holding a bundle of something, a bundle of hessian of the sort used for making sandbags or temporary windbreaks. For some reason, when he first saw it, the Dogger thought the man was holding a baby.

Over afternoon tea with Marj, excess saliva suddenly springs into Linda's mouth, too much for the mere ginger nut biscuit she is bringing to her lips. A hot, prickly sensation sweeps over her. Pregnancy. She looks at Marj, feeling she could vomit the truth at any moment. So she keeps her mouth shut and waits for the sensation to pass.

The sun goes down in a blaze of orange and pink and yellow and grey. It's a moonless night. There is a low, deep growl, possibly a moan, emanating from the black holes out in space.

*

Out over the starlit sea, humpback whales pass by the town, singing. The One Mile Jetty reaches out towards them, but they're much further out, past the islands. The whales swim parallel to the coast, mothers with calves, their throats covered in barnacles and teeming lice. Phosphorus swirls around them like moving cities seen from a passing satellite.

Linda Johnson stands at her kitchen sink at midnight, grating yellow Sunlight soap over boiling tea towels. The yellow gratings drop gently down onto the blue-and-white-checked fabric. The refrigerator hums. Linda is boiling her tea towels in a big pot over a gently hissing gas burner. Bubbles gently rise under the fabric, creating heaving bosoms. Linda pokes at them with a wooden spoon, drowning them under soapy boiling water.

The bulging fabric rises up taut over a lump of air. A tiny mote of soap dust drops gently down. The soap strikes the fabric with infinitesimal force, but strikes it with more force than all the radio waves striking all the radio telescope dishes in the world. The refrigerator stops with a little shudder of its rounded shoulders, creating a sensation of absolute silence in Linda's kitchen.

Linda empties her hot tea towels into the sink and runs cold water over them. She wrings them out and pegs them on the line, under the stars.

She dreams one of her recurring dreams. She is standing in a line, the sort of line you stand in when you're buying tickets to see a movie. The destination is a kiln with an open mouth. The line shuffles forward every time someone goes in. This is not the only line; there are lines of people as far as the eye can see to left and right, and each line is inching towards its own kiln. But people are not visibly distressed. The atmosphere is one of passive resignation. Linda, just a child, turns to her mother and asks, 'Why are we standing in this line? Why don't we run for it?' Her mother looks slightly annoyed by the question, as if the answer were obvious. She shrugs and says, 'Well, everyone else is going in.' And then Linda tries to scream, but no scream comes out, just the tiniest little rasp, and it is always at this point that she wakes up.

***

I wake with a start, feeling that something is terribly wrong. I open my eyes, flick my neck – as I do after a long sleep – and look at the floor.

It is morning at last. The cyclone has passed, and it is time to survey the wreckage. There, below me, are the shredded remains of Lizzie's precious hardcover collectable book, *The Lore of the Lyrebird*.

How could I have been so stupid? How could I have given in to temptation so easily? I remonstrate with myself. *Stupid dickhead.* I'll have to charm my way out of this one. A lot of charm, a lot of pathos.

I begin to croon. 'Oh, poor Lucky. Oh, poor Lucky!'

I say it aloud, in English, not caring if I wake Lizzie. She'll come out and see what I've done. She'll be angry. It's best to get it over with.

But she stays in bed, sleeping off her threnody.

If I could, I'd clean up the mess myself. But I can't. A captive galah can never clean up her own mess. She can never stop *making* a mess.

TEN

To the moon

LINDA AND JO meet Evan off the plane. Three months is a proportionally large part of Jo's life; she has almost forgotten her father. But when she sees him it all comes rushing back. She reaches for him, curls her arms around his neck.

Linda's great need is to convert the unofficial child inside her into a plausibly official one. Evan is surprised and delighted by her overtures.

They name their new daughter Stella, in honour of outer space. Linda is not so sure about this – she can't help but think of Marlon Brando shouting the name – but she is not in a position to argue. When Stella is born, Linda says the baby was premature, in case anyone decides to do the maths. Evan accepts this explanation. Doubt might have tried to creep in, after dark, but it is shunned. It is not entertained with even the tiniest drip of Emu Bitter or crumb of Jatz biscuit. Stella Johnson, bearing his name on the label fixed to the underside of the lid of her tiny kindergarten case, looking up at him, asking him questions, can only be his daughter. At work, he is known as a man with a *wife and kids*. It's all very simple, really.

Similarly, the Moon Landing may seem complex, but at its heart lie the sturdy maxims of Newtonian physics. To leave earth's orbit, all that is necessary is to reach escape velocity: the minimum speed necessary to overcome the gravitational pull of the earth. The formula can be expressed thus:

$$v_e = \sqrt{\frac{2GM}{r}},$$

where G is the universal gravitational constant ($G = 6.67 \times 10^{-11}$ m^3 kg^{-1} s^{-2}), M the mass of the body to be escaped, and r the distance from the centre of mass of the object.

Tracking stations around the earth are now sending and receiving signals from spaceships named after the Greek gods: Mercury, Gemini, Apollo. One explodes on earth, causing temporary confusion and dismay. But others succeed, and become ever more audacious.

In December 1968, three astronauts set off to fly all the way around the moon for the first time. They immediately come down with the flu. The muscles in their weightless bodies eject waste from various orifices. Pulsating balls of vomit float around the cabin.

'You're riding the best bird we can find,' says Houston, to cheer them up.

As the astronauts near LOS – Loss of Signal behind the moon – Evan and his colleagues stare, transfixed, as all the lights go out on their console. Communications have ceased. Three human beings are alone on the other side of the moon. The disconnection is absolute. Can it be survived? Perhaps this was a mistake. A giant, expensive mistake. The trackers sit it out, not daring to speak, waiting for the lights to come back on. When they do, the trackers cheer. It was not a mistake. It can be done.

So, what was it like, around the back of the moon?

Nothing special, says astronaut William Anders. 'The backside looks like a sand pile my kids have played in for some time. It's all beat up, no definition, just a lot of bumps and holes.'

Stella Johnson holds a cat's-eye marble to her eye and sees how the world can curve and distort. She notices the differing qualities – of colour and taste, despite similarity in texture – between the green and the red jelly wobbling in her dessert bowl. She is aware that the fridge sometimes falls silent, creating an intensity of silence that is almost overwhelming.

Whenever she gets a chance, she asks her father questions. Why is the sky blue? How do clouds stay up there? He answers patiently and accurately. The answers don't entirely satisfy her, because she doesn't understand them, so she asks another question and another, hoping to get to the bottom of something.

Despite his denials, she believes that he is an astronaut. She thinks he changes into his astronaut suit when he gets to work. He flies up to the moon and back within a workday, changing back into ordinary clothes before he comes home in the twelve-seater van.

When Evan is unavailable, which is most of the time, she directs her questions to Linda or, as a last resort, to Jo.

With Jo at school, Stella and Linda like to break up their day by spending time at the Kellys' place. Stella is often left to mingle with the younger Kellys while Linda goes off to do some shopping or a few errands.

'A committee meeting,' says Linda.

Marjorie nods, and Linda might be gone for hours; much longer than a committee meeting. The extra child is absorbed among her own, and doesn't eat much.

One day, at his console, with his earphones on, Evan feels a little push from his colleague, causing his chair to swivel. He catches sight of his younger daughter just inside the doorway, loses his grumpy expression and opens his arms to her. She has been brought to see Daddy's work for herself, to correct her belief that he works on the moon.

She comes trotting across the room, and he lifts her onto his lap, telling her she can't touch anything. 'I know,' she sighs. She looks at the knobs and switches, greedily taking them all in, imagining her fingers on them. Evan gently spins the chair all the way around, like the spinning of earth on its axis. Once, twice, three times, but no more. And then, slightly dizzy and listing, she is trotting back across the room and out the door, and he is turning back to his console.

For now, Evan Johnson has time. He has no idea it is precious. He considers it infinitely available, like water in the ocean. Here at the tracking station, his task is to measure and manage it, to deliver it up in useful mathematical equations. He enjoys this work enormously. As soon as Stella slides off his chair, this work refills his mind.

There is a Casper comic on the brown carpet near Jo Johnson's feet. A wooden pencil case is fanned open at her elbow revealing sharpened-down coloured pencils in varying lengths. She is lying belly-down, looking at the crisp new *How and Why Wonder Book* Linda has just given her. The word *STARS* is printed in bold white type on the front cover.

As Linda pads barefoot to the couch, Jo restrains herself from opening the book until she has properly studied the cover. She examines the photograph of a long, smooth, light-grey telescope floating in pitch-black space, surrounded by a speckle of white dots. After she has finished studying the cover, taking note of the price (sixty-nine cents), she turns the page and sees a boy and girl looking heavenwards, surrounded by a blue watercolour puddle of sky and more white star-dots. The boy has his mouth open, smiling so hard he might be laughing. The little blonde girl beside him is unsmiling, wide-eyed and slightly bewildered. While the secrets of the universe will reveal themselves easily to her confident, laughing brother, it might take a little longer for the sister to catch on.

Jo has a little sister just like this one. She likes the way Stella looks up at her trustingly with wide hazel eyes, a little sprinkle of freckles over her nose and little translucent plastic green balls, called bobbles, holding her hair in pigtails on each side of her head. Sometimes, though, Stella is exceedingly irritating, and Jo has to tell her to *scram*.

Like her father, Jo takes a systematic approach to her studies. She reads books from cover to cover, in the order that the pages are given, never (like Linda, for example) sneaking a look at the ending or a random point halfway through. She even makes herself read the boring pages at the beginning. This book is by Norman Hoss and Illustrated by James Ponter. It is Edited under the Supervision of Dr Paul E. Blackwood, Washington D.C. and it has been Approved by – hey, can that really be a man's name? Jo is pleased to have found the first thing that needs explaining. She gets up, book in hand, to ask Evan.

Evan is sitting on the floor on the other side of the room, wearing headphones, listening to whatever it is going around and around on the record player. Jo sits down cross-legged beside him. Evan's eyes are shut and he is frowning slightly, nodding slightly, but these only serve to accentuate his essential stillness. Evan becomes aware of a presence and opens his eyes. He puts a finger up to make Jo wait. He carefully lifts the needle by means of a tiny lever, and pulls his headphones off his ears, letting them hug his neck. The glossy black record continues to spin, the needle hanging half an inch above it. Evan is happy to interrupt his music to talk with Jo about stars. He gets ready to explain some-thing. All he needs is a question.

'Dad, is this a man's name?'

Jo keeps her finger on the book as Evan tries to turn it around to get a proper look.

'Let go of it, Jo, I can see the bit you mean.'

Text and illustrations approved by Oakes A. White
Brooklyn Children's Museum
Brooklyn, New York

'Yes, Oakes is the man's first name. His last name is White.'

'An oak is a type of tree, isn't it?'

'That's right. But this is just someone's name, it has nothing to do with a tree.'

'What does the A stand for, Dad?'

Jo knows this is a stupid question, but it's too late now.

'How am I supposed to know that?' says Evan sharply. But then he softens, keeping the conversation going.

'It could be Anthony, or Andrew. It could be anything starting with the letter A.'

'Oakes Anything White,' quips Linda from the couch.

'Americans have funny names,' says Jo.

She is thinking of a couple of visiting NASA men who came to the house for a barbecue. They were *Chad* and *Mitch* and they asked for *ketchup*.

'How do you like the book?' asks Evan. 'Is there anything you don't understand?'

'I'm only up to this page,' says Jo, pointing at the upward-looking boy and girl.

Evan puts his headphones back on, lowers the needle and is instantly reabsorbed into the music. Jo wishes she had come over with a more interesting, longer-lasting question.

191

The white dots on the black background on the book of *STARS* remind Linda of an advertisement for anti-dandruff shampoo she had seen in *Reader's Digest*. In the middle of the page there was a plain black square over which the reader was invited to lower his or her head while scratching his or her scalp. Linda did this and saw the white dots appear on the black square. She saw that she had dandruff. After she had completed this experiment, she brushed her dandruff off into the air, letting it land wherever it would.

Stella watches Mrs Kelly grating yellow cheese over a pot of simmering water.

'Why are you grating cheese over the tea towels, Mrs Kelly?'

Stella is laughed at – from all corners of the room – for this misapprehension.

'It's soap, pet,' says Mrs Kelly, holding out the bar. 'Have a sniff.'

But now there's another question.

'Why do you always boil things?' Stella is sitting at the Kelly dining table as if she were a member of the family, impertinently firing questions across the room. Mr Kelly is there, brooding over a cup of tea.

'It's because she's an old boiler,' he says slowly, looking Stella straight in the eye.

Another gale of laugher.

Mrs Kelly says, 'Oh shoosh up, Kev! I'll give you old boiler.'

'Doesn't *your* Mum boil tea towels?' asks Susan.

'No,' said Stella. 'She just puts them in the washing machine.'

'Everything together?' asks Susan. 'Hankies, pants, everything?'

Now Stella can't be sure. 'Yes.'

'She doesn't even boil the snotty hankies?'

'No.'

Susan widens her eyes and retails a bit of her mother's philosophy: 'You shouldn't mix germs. You shouldn't mix pants germs with hanky germs.'

'Susan!' says Mrs Kelly. 'People can do their washing however they want.'

'But you said! Never mix pants germs with hanky germs!'

'What did I just tell you, Susan? Do you want a smack on the bottom?'

A pause.

'Now we're cooking with gas,' says Mr Kelly. He has a collection of phrases he uses here and there. His voice is soggy; he is wearing the white singlet that speaks of sleep.

'I'm taking my tea into the sewing room and don't try to follow me,' says Mrs Kelly to all present. 'Don't let it boil dry.'

With Mrs Kelly gone there is a sense of freedom, of the loosening of bonds, but also a loss of leadership, of not knowing quite what to do next. Mr Kelly adds another teaspoon of sugar to his tea, and stirs.

Susan and Stella go out into the backyard, behind the toilet.

'Let's swear,' says Stella. 'You go first.'

'Bum,' says Susan, her eyes darting.

'Bum,' says Stella.

They looked at each other quizzically. Not as thrilling as expected.

Then they hear Kevin Kelly's voice: 'How can I dance with a little girl on my foot?'

They come around from the back of the toilet to see Kevin Kelly with a little straggly-haired girl standing on his feet, her small bare feet curled over his large bare feet. They're dancing, hand in hand.

I'm watching from my cage. I'm dancing, too.

Linda Johnson is boiling tea towels and snotty handker-chiefs late at night, after the children have gone to bed. She is smoking a cigarette, drinking coffee, reading 'Life's Like That' in *Reader's Digest*. Evan is, as usual these days, working very late. She rinses the steaming items under cold water in the sink and hangs them out on the clothesline in the soft air of night, under a star-rich sky. When Stella wakes up in the morning the handkerchiefs and tea towels will already be there, pegged out on the line, unremarked, unremarkable. Stella will be none the wiser.

Linda doesn't go to bed just yet. She takes paper and pencil and makes sketches for her Moon Ball dress. It will be silver and shimmery, to suggest the moon itself. But it should not look too much like a theatrical costume; it must still be elegant. Perhaps there will be a split up the side to show off a long brown leg. Her hair will be piled on top of her head in a series of artful curls. Or perhaps not. Perhaps left long and loose or in a low ponytail – shades of the bohemian, of Greenwich Village. Or perhaps not.

Linda Johnson is not the only woman in Port Badminton thinking about outfit and hair, of course.

In the days before the Moon Ball, the town's hairdressers will be run off their feet. Afterwards, the ladies will preserve their hairdos for as long as possible by going to bed with satin scarves wrapped around their heads, or by using satin pillows. They will then be seen going about their usual business in casual slacks and flat shoes with hair that is still magnificently 'up', though gradually subsiding. To wash and brush it out immediately after the ball would be considered a waste.

In just a few years' time, Linda will throw all of this aside, declare herself a feminist, study sociology as a mature-aged student. But in 1969, shortly before the Moon Landing, she's still working hard at Normal. A glossy, perfect Normal.

The Johnsons suddenly disappear. Their car is still sitting beside the house but Jo and Stella aren't there. Marj tells Susan they've gone to see relatives in Melbourne; they'll be back soon. *Soon* is no good to Susan. She stands on Clam Street looking down the road, waiting for Stella and Jo to return.

Marj says: 'They'll be back, Poppet,' and then, 'What's wrong with your sister? Play with your sister.'

Susan looks at her younger sister with her inferior hand–eye coordination and refuses. The snubbed sister cries. Susan continues to stand at the gate, alone, waiting.

195

While they are away, Marj takes her into the Johnsons' house to water the houseplants. They acknowledge the revered car that Susan was born in and enter through the back door. Marjorie fills the watering can in the laundry, looking absently at Linda's dried-out mop. Everything seems impossibly clean and new and ordered.

Marj stands before each potted plant, worrying about giving it too much or too little. The house is silent, slightly unnerving. Evan's expensive stereo player sits on the floor on a thick cream rug. There are books on the bookshelves, including an entire *Encylopaedia Britannica*, yellow-spined *National Geographics* and a row of *Reader's Digests*. A glazed ceramic ashtray seems ugly to Marjorie, but she trusts that it must be *the in thing*. She decides to buy one like it.

A vase sits low on a coffee table of polished teak in a position that could not be countenanced in the Kelly household. It would be swished off by child or animal in two minutes, break into pieces on the floor. The coffee table itself would quickly drown in miscellaneous items: a pile of clean underpants brought in from the clothesline, pages out of the *Northern Times*, a large clamshell being used as a bed for a small doll. Marjorie allows Susan to look at things but not touch. Susan's eyes are drawn to the giant wooden fork and spoon on the wall above the head of the dining table. She finds them spooky. She would find it difficult to eat her dinner with this giant cutlery looming over her.

They make the most of these visits because they don't often see the inside of the Johnsons' place: social intercourse between the two families mainly takes place at the Kellys', where there are no ceramic vases on low coffee tables to tip over and it is a good place to corral noisy children that might wake up Evan Johnson, who often works overnight shifts and needs to sleep during the day.

Susan is putting her doll to bed in the clamshell when Kevin calls her.

'Susan! Your little playmates are back!'

Susan goes rushing out of the house and there they are, Stella and Jo, in all their returned glory.

While they were away in Melbourne, Stella and Jo had watched television. They saw *Adventure Island* and *Skippy*. The Kellys have never seen television, other than pictures in *The Women's Weekly*.

'And we saw ads,' says Jo.

'What's an ad?' asks Susan.

'Don't you know?' says Jo smugly.

Jo has a mental image of an ad, but she is not sure how to explain it. So she describes it.

'There was a lady having a bath in lemonade,' she says. 'People were standing around her with jugs, pouring in the lemonade.'

'Did she sip it?' asks Susan.

'She didn't drink any, she was just having a bath.'

The Kelly and Johnson children are a pack. They have gradually expanded their range beyond Clam Street and have begun to tour the outer reaches of the boggy samphire flat and make unsupervised forays to the seawall. When they get back Mrs Kelly lines up plastic cups and sloshes green or red cordial into them. She'll hand them out, saying things like, 'There y'are, pet,' or, 'Don't gulp it!' or, 'What do you say?'

'Thank you.'

Sometimes Kevin Kelly will look at them all: seven girls. How can there be so many girls? He had imagined boys – one boy at least – to go fishing with.

The girls come down with chicken pox, each with a rash of red spots on the belly. They lift their skirts to compare notes. Other ailments come and go, sometimes simultaneously, sometimes overlapping or at different times: diarrhoea, vomiting, sores, scabs, burns, a nose so runny and afflicted it is not just snotting but bleeding, forming scabs to be picked off. Boils. Midge bites that must be painted with calamine lotion. Doublegees in the feet, hot sand and bitumen burning the soles. Sand in the crotch of bathers. The peeling of sunburn. The discomfort when sleeping with a severe case of sunburn. Eyelids swelling up from being so thoroughly sunburned.

The Johnson and Kelly children don't go to school together. They all set off together from Clam Street, but the Kellys turn off in the direction of the Catholic school; Jo walks on, stepping through the gates of the state primary school.

From time to time, Jo feels socially obliged to stand at the stone wall of the Convent – that's what the state school children call the Catholic school – chanting 'ConDOGS! ConDOGS!' At first she stands back, puzzled. But over time, she discovers that it is like barracking for one's sports team or using the correct colours in a scribble pattern: some things in life are governed by the spirit of the hive. Shouting her Condogs, Jo catches the eye of a Kelly girl and falters.

'State, State, fulla HATE!' shrieks the Kelly. The quick look she gives Jo says: *Don't worry, it's just a game.*

They play together after school as usual.

When they hear the trackers' minibus, Susan's face clouds over. She never wants Jo and Stella to go home. She hangs on to an elbow, or stands in the doorway to block their exit. She watches them scamper off to receive Evan as the door rolls back and he steps out.

DISH: Stand by. Incoming rueful thoughts Jo Johnson.
GALAH: Roger.

JO JOHNSON: When I try to conjure up his face, all I can see is a black-and-white photograph that was taken not long after we arrived in Port Badminton. He is sitting at his console full of knobs and dials. His face, behind his horn-rimmed glasses, is in three-quarter profile because he has swivelled around on his chair to discuss something with a colleague. He is wearing a long-sleeved white shirt with a dark tie. There is a biro hooked over his pocket. This is not a memory of my father; it's a memory of a photograph of my father.

I'd run to watch him get out of the minibus. He'd be parting with his colleagues in a little effusion of banter and jokes, always ended by the roll and slam of the sliding door. Then I'd be at him, asking questions, telling him things. The interval between the end of the school day and my father's return from work was long and lavish. It was like a second day with its own beginning, middle and end. I spent a lot of this time playing with the Kelly kids from next-door-but-one.

I knew Susan was watching wistfully as I ran to meet my father. Hers was away for weeks at a time on a prawn trawler, or, more likely, at the pub getting drunk. I'd leave the friendly noise and chaos of her house and enter mine, all neat and ordered, holding my father's large warm hand. I had a room to myself. On the rare occasion she came into the house, Susan would stand in the middle of my room, marvelling at all the space I had just to myself. She'd hold out her arms and spin on the spot to relish it. She'd say, 'Is that your own doll? Is that your own picture?' And I'd say yes, yes, it was all mine, mine alone. I had a long-limbed clown doll sitting just so on a cream chenille bedspread. There was a lamb's wool rug on the cool polished floorboards. I had a white mirrored dressing table with a little metal stool before it – not really for sitting on – upon which there was a fuzzy purple cushion.

I had a low bookcase with a row of Vegemite jars on it containing tiny specimens. There was a baby crab claw and shells collected from the beach at the Blowholes; the scaly sloughed-off skin of the leg of a skink, a dry piece of kangaroo vertebrae with red dust clinging to it. A piece of dark yellow mookaite rock that looked like broken toffee, edible. A nasturtium seed sprouting in wet cotton wool. A dead beetle with a brim all the way around it like the brim of a hat. A doublegee had lodged in my heel. It, too, had been given a place in a jar and labelled. If you looked closely, you could see how the end of one of the spines was darkened with my blood.

I had a small microscope for looking at a hair, or the big juicy cells of an onion, or a drop of water from a puddle in which translucent beings jerked around in a little world of their own.

Susan would look solemnly at each thing in turn. Later, we asked Mrs Kelly for a spare jar, so Susan could put a specimen in it.

'To put what in, pet?'

'A pebble, or a prickle,' said Susan.

'I can't spare a jar but you can have a tin to play with,' said Mrs Kelly.

We weren't playing. This was *science*.

I saw how Susan, disappointed, took the tin and put a pebble in it and found it wanting.

Sometimes I'd give Susan something out of my room – a tiny pink doll's pram, for example – and she'd run home with it immediately, keen to show off her prize.

Susan's things were shared among five girls. The floor of their room – they all slept in one small room – seemed to be permanently littered with small pieces of old broken toys. There would be a pink plastic doll's arm, a head somewhere else; marbles to roll underfoot and trip you up so that you landed on your bottom and were laughed at; the wheel of a tricycle; stuffing out of a teddy bear. Sometimes the Kelly girls would tidy up by simply sweeping everything under the beds.

The oldest girl had a bed to herself; the other four slept at either end of two single beds. The room was a bit smelly –

a lot of wet sheets passed through it – with sweeter notes, possibly biscuit crumbs or strawberry jam.

I can't remember them having a cupboard in there. Where did they keep their clothes? I do remember an old wicker basket full of washing that lived on the kitchen table. It would be put on the floor before a meal, then hoisted back up again afterwards.

DISH: Over.
GALAH: Roger.

Evan and Jo are sitting at the table, drawing circles. Some are worked using a compass, others, wobbly, are hand-drawn. They draw three circles, barely touching but not intersecting. In the curved space left between the three circles Evan directs Jo to draw a small circle which touches all three big circles – again, just grazing them – and then a circle all the way around the outside. These are the inner and outer soddy circles.

Linda, who is drying dishes, gets snagged on the word *soddy*.

'Oh, sod it!' cries Linda, throwing down the tea towel. She puts milk into a saucepan for cocoa.

Stella joins in: 'Sod it! Sod it!'

Evan patiently waits this out. His wife and younger daughter are so easily distracted. Their thoughts move messily all around their brains, brains in which work and play and geometry and tea towels merge and bleed into each other.

Jo, on the other hand, has been listening carefully. She tunes her ears to her father's voice. If they could swivel around to listen better, they would. She draws her soddy circles.

He explains that within the gasket, you can draw more and more circles between and lightly touching the other circles, 'but eventually, you do reach the end – you can't draw any more circles.'

Evan's relief at this sparkles quietly in his eyes.

'What about infinity?' asks Jo.

'What about it?' asks Evan.

Jo likes infinity. That is all. But it's hard to explain. And she is wondering if, perhaps, you could draw more circles going infinitely small into infinity forever, only you're stuck because of the width of the lead in your pencil.

'No,' says Evan firmly. 'The Apollonian Gasket is finite. You have tiny, tiny circles but in the end, you get to a circle with a zero radius – which of course is not a circle, so just before that, you have the last circle.'

All circles accounted for, even if only theoretically.

Jo imagines drawing tinier and tinier circles within the outer soddy circle, drawing until she had drawn all possible circles and can put down her pencil and be satisfied.

'Oh, sod it!' cries Linda, for real this time, as the milk boils over and goes everywhere.

Jo's feet are leathery and tough. Her feet grow rapidly, big for her age. Out of school, she wears them bare or in rubber thongs. At the heel, the ball of the foot and the big toe, the rubber is beginning to wear down through the white upper layer to show the blue lower layer. She imagines her thongs in cross-section and thinks of sediment, of rock layers.

She likes to peel things and lift things up. In the bathroom, she picks at the fish-themed Con-Tact wall and bench coverings Linda has laboured to apply smoothly, without trapping bubbles. She finds an edge and lifts it with a fingernail, knowing this will annoy but unable to resist.

In this ninth year of her life – she will turn nine after the Moon Landing – her goal is to collect a complete Crazy Camel Train set, the various parts of which are to be found in cellophane packets in Kellogg's Cornflakes boxes. At the supermarket, she tries to herd Linda towards the breakfast cereals, lingering there, looking at the boxes as if she could use X-ray vision to see the tiny toys inside.

At impossibly long intervals, Linda buys a new box of cornflakes, usually while Jo is at school, when she has temporarily forgotten all about her project. Then one morning she will be surprised by a new box on the table, set in front of her place, waiting for her. At these times there will always be a small consolation prize for Stella, who has for the duration of the camel train era conceded cereal box rights to her sister. Stella might get a hairclip, or a five-cent piece, or even a tiny pink plastic pram for the tiniest pink baby doll. Jo will sit before the cereal box for a moment, as if in prayer, before opening it up. She uses a butter knife to cut around the top of the box, and then she is allowed to lift out the wax-paper bag containing the cornflakes – Linda can fit that back in later – and reach down to the bottom of the box, fingers closing over the cellophane. Everyone watches, interested, as she draws it out, eyes shut, holding it in the palm of her hand, then opening a screwed-up eye just a bit, a little bit more, to see.

The complete camel train consists of an engine in front, running on camel pedal-power, followed by a first-class compartment in which a single monkey in a top hat sits on a single hump under a sumptuous fringed canopy, a sleeping car sporting a bed perched atop a sitting camel, and a four-humped economy-class camel bearing three lower-income monkeys. There is a signal box to be put off to one side of the track, next to a monkey holding two flags. Coming up the rear, there is the guard's van, with a camel kneeling on a trunk no doubt full of interesting paraphernalia, if you could only move the camel, lift the lid (but you can't, because they're made of a single piece of moulded plastic).

Jo has so far collected part of the engine in green, the signal box in red and the four-humped economy class camel in orange. She needs the first-class camel and various accessories. Most of all, she needs the sleeping compartment camel and monkey, which come separately. The monkey is sitting up in bed wearing a nightcap, eating a banana. There is a hook on the bed for a tiny bedpan, and the bedpan itself. She imagines herself in bed atop the gently swaying hump of a camel, rolling on camel train tracks through the desert night, falling in and out of sleep. One would wake up to see the stars, then wake again to see the dawn.

Jo opens her eyes and her face falls. She lets the small cellophane packet drop onto the placemat beside her Skippy milk cup.

'What is it?' asks Stella.

'A signal box,' says Jo.

'Better luck next time,' says Evan.

Evan stands at the front of the house waiting for the minibus. He, too, is disappointed, for Jo and also for himself. He'd quite like to see the complete set.

Back in the house, Jo's fingers are itching to tear open the cellophane and start pressing the plastic pieces out of their plastic frame. She decides to keep the unopened packet for swapping.

In her quest for camel train pieces, Jo eats two bowls of cornflakes every morning. The sooner the box empties, the sooner another box will be bought. She would eat even more, but Linda stops her.

One day, in the toilet, she gets an idea. She doesn't have to eat her way through the cornflakes. She can cut out the process in the middle, the passage of cornflakes down the alimentary canal and out into the world at the other end. She can pour cereal straight down the toilet and flush it away.

If she pours too much down the toilet, it will be noticed. She must be careful. She thinks up a scheme to get rid of small amounts at a time: a Skippy cupful here, a handful there. She decides to get out of bed and sneak into the kitchen in the middle of the night. But she forgets all about her plan, and sleeps through the night.

On their next run, the astronauts wear new extravehicular mobility units, or EMUs. The EMUs provide a complete life-support system, allowing astronauts to escape the umbilical cord of their spaceship.

The EMUs are sewn together by a team led by Eleanor Foraker at her machine in Delaware, USA, using ordinary Singer sewing machines.

They stitch together a Nomex comfort layer next to the skin, then a neoprene-coated nylon pressure bladder, a nylon restraint layer, seven layers of Beta/Kapton spacer laminate and an outer layer of Teflon-coated Beta fabric.

The great danger lies in stray sewing pins. Just one pin accidentally left inside the suit could spell disaster, puncturing the layers and killing the astronaut inside. Eleanor Foraker must track and account for every pin used by her team.

Under all the layers of his EMU, the astronaut is obliged to wear adult incontinence nappies, of the kind that can be bought from an ordinary supermarket.

In Port Badminton, Western Australia, Marjorie Kelly gets to work on Linda's Moon Ball gown. She is to be Artemis, sister of Apollo. It *is* a rather theatrical idea, but the first moon landing will only ever happen once. What about accoutrements – a bow and quiver? No, that would be silly. The date of the ball is set down for August, some weeks after the Moon Landing itself, so as not to distract.

I was in my cage, staring at the back door, when Linda Johnson burst through it. She came past in a silver shimmer, a swirl of light that emerged on the dry grass of the backyard.

Her hair is piled loosely on top of her head, threatening to fall. Soft tendrils of escaping hair follow her head, wafting in the air about her face and neck. She twirls around in front of her audience of Mrs Kelly, Jo, Stella, various little Kelly girls, and me. Her arms and neck are long and of uniform colour – quite different to the Kellys', which are shorter, freckled and prone to sunburn. Stella applauds, her open palms splatting together.

'Of course, I won't be wearing these silly sandals,' says Linda, looking down at them.

We all look at her feet: flat brown sandals, almost the same colour as her flesh.

'What sort of shoes would set it off?' asks Mrs Kelly.

'I know!' says Linda, holding out a foot. 'I could go over these with silver paint.'

'Silver paint!' gasps a Kelly girl.

At this, I begin to screech. I screech blue murder. I have my claws wrapped around the ceiling of the cage, head pointing downwards. I throw my head back and forth, making myself dizzy.

'Shoosh up, cocky,' says Mrs Kelly. 'What's all that racket?'

I'm jealous, simple as that. I have no mother, no siblings, no ball gown, no glittery button. I am lonely and stuck in a cage. I have never fledged or flown. I cannot even stretch out my wings. I will never get out of this wretched cage.

I go silent, hanging upside down, looking down at my own droppings.

Mrs Johnson goes back inside. Mrs Kelly and all the daughters trail her like courtiers.

Later, Marj and her daughters discuss Linda's beautiful dress and the beauty of Linda Johnson herself.

'She doesn't have blonde hair though,' says the oldest Kelly girl. 'Gentlemen prefer blondes.'

'Well,' says Marjorie firmly, 'brunettes can be just as beautiful as blondes.'

'Yes,' agree most of the other Kelly girls.

All the Kelly girls, like their father, have ginger hair, neither blonde nor brunette.

Two American astronauts, along with their wives and a NASA public relations man, are guests of honour at the Port Badminton Tropical Festival. They are met by Crowie at the airport, along with the *Northern Times* reporter and the tracking station Cap Com. The guests are accommodated in sagging single beds at the Port Hotel and given fried tomatoes for breakfast. The tomatoes touch their bacon and eggs, tainting them.

'A fried tomato is not something we'd have for breakfast in the States,' says the PR man, to explain the lightly-touched food. The girl picking up their plates just shrugs.

The hungry guests are invited to stand on the back of a flatbed truck for the festival parade. They'll be able to hold on to the railing with one hand, and wave to the crowd with the other. The truck lurches suddenly into motion, making them all flail for the railing.

They hold on tight with both hands, and therefore fail to wave. But they do flash big smiles with their straight white teeth. The townspeople of Port Badminton line the road in a straggle all the way from the seawall to the Pony Club. The truck is preceded by a self-important white ute which brakes unexpectedly from time to time, causing the guests to jostle one another. Small children are disappointed. They look like ordinary people. Where are their spacesuits?

Behind the astronauts' truck, there are four camels with studiedly bored-looking teenagers riding on their humps. Then there is the hospital's float with a cross-eyed doctor wielding a giant scalpel and splashings of red paint all around, and then there are guitar-strumming Girl Guides among blue crepe-paper rosettes, mouths opening and shutting, their thin voices lost in the wind; and then a squad of Pony Club horses with their tails neatly plaited and one of them skittish, skipping sideways out of line. The fire brigade, the softball team, bales of wool, a boat decorated with fishing nets and captured cardboard prawns and alfoil fish glinting in the sun all glide by.

The ute abruptly swings left off the bitumen, kicking up a cloud of dust that settles over the faces of the important visitors. Each feels the grit crunching between his or her teeth. The assault is so thorough and so sudden that they wonder, for an instant, if they are being deliberately insulted. Each eats his dust alone, staring fixedly ahead. The truck stops. The dust clears. They are at the Pony Club. In no hurry, the ute and truck drivers sit where they are. The visitors look at each other, their faces covered in dust, and laugh.

They are treated to a civic dinner of lamb and mint sauce and a speech by the mayor.

'Why do they call him Crowbar?' asks the NASA public relations man.

A town councillor swallows a mouthful of beer and explains: 'He owns the pub, the Port Badminton Hotel. An Abo – an Aborigine – was kicking up a stink so he hit him with a piece of coax cable.'

'Coax cable?'

'You know – coaxial cable.'

'Yes, I do know coaxial cable. So why do they call him Crowbar?'

'Well, everyone thinks he used a crowbar, but I have a mate who was there that night and it was only a piece of coax cable.'

The public relations man chews his lamb thoughtfully.

'It was about yay long,' says the town councillor, giving a gesture of measurement, the way people do when they are describing the length of a fish.

Five, four, three, two, one – BLAST OFF! The children's arms are the fins of rocket ships. There is fairy floss at the festival, and displays of mangoes. The flat carriages that used to take wool out to the end of the One Mile Jetty have been brought here and laid out in a circle, within which ponies are jumped and put through their paces. Children run around and around atop the carriages, leaping over metal and wood, sometimes cutting their knees.

There are also giant wooden cotton reels to play on: the reels that brought the coaxial cable into town. Children run backwards on the spot on them, making the reels roll forwards.

*

Jo is a Brownie Guide. She has learned her Promise and gets through her Promise Ceremony without a hitch. She is careful to touch knees on both sides with her fellow Brownies when they go into powwow, so that their secrets can't escape.

At the end of each session, the entire pack faces its leaders, salutes and sings: 'Goodnight, Brown Owl! Goodnight, Tawny Owl! Goodnight, Pack Leader and goodnight, everyone!'

Still singing, they turn and start skipping towards the door. The pack emerges out of the front door of the weatherboard hall and disperses into the waiting cars of parents.

At home, she tends the tadpoles she has collected from the ponds at the bottom of the levee banks. Linda boils cabbage leaves, allows them to cool, and helps Jo lower them down over the tadpoles. Their mouths are like tiny black rubber bands. They already have buds where their hind legs will grow.

When Jo and Linda get home from Brownies one afternoon, they find Susan Kelly and Stella Johnson at the gate, their faces swollen from crying. A brief question-and-answer session establishes that Susan wants to be a Brownie too, but her mother has said No, and Stella wants to be a Brownie, but her mother, also, has said No.

'When you're older you can be a Brownie!' says Linda to Stella. Susan's exclusion is more complicated.

Kevin Kelly has been off work with a bad back. He has been staying out late at the Port Hotel, coming home dead drunk, then lying around the house during the day, snoring and jerking suddenly awake. There is barely a cent to get food on the table, much less berets and gold badges and fawn socks and whatnot. It might be all right if it were just Susan, but if Susan goes, the others will want to go. This is not information Marjorie had intended to make public, at least not this bluntly, but Susan doesn't care. She relays all of it, hiccupping and blowing her nose. Her disappointment at missing out on Brownies is beyond family loyalty, beyond shame.

Jo, in her crisp but very hot Brownie uniform, watches this grovelling performance, slightly appalled. But Linda, remembering her own outcast childhood, is thinking up a scheme. The next afternoon, a Wednesday, she plays Brown Owl for a special Clam Street Brownie pack made up of all the Kelly girls and Stella and Jo. Jo is not to wear her uniform for this: like the others, she must participate in civvies and wear paper badges.

They all sit in a powwow and say the Brownie Guide promise. The little Kelly girls push each other to sit on either side of Linda.

Linda knows her father, champion of the less fortunate, would be proud of her.

Susan has fun in Linda's pack but she still covets a real uniform, a real beret, a real pair of fawn socks. When she grows up, she would like to be rich.

ELEVEN

The Moon Landing

It is just after four in the morning on Monday, 21 July 1969, Florida time.

Three male human beings consume steak, scrambled eggs and toast. They drink orange juice and coffee.

After breakfast, they walk down a long corridor to their change room. They strip naked. Their bodies have evolved from the first multi-celled organisms, the first organisms to propel themselves independently, the first organisms to grow spines and limbs, through the fish stage of a blue watery planet, through simian stages high in the branches of trees and thence down to the golden African plains, walking on two back legs, muscles rippling under almost hairless skin. And now they will leave the blue and green womb of the earth and set their feet down on other soil. This can only be done in the right clothes. Without the right clothes, their bodies will melt down or freeze over; they will be dead in seconds.

In the change room, their naked bodies are wired up with medical sensors and communication equipment.

Attendants move around them the way Afghan cameleers moved about the camels, hitching things up, adding things on. The layers sewn by Mrs Foraker and her industrious team are bundled over the bodies of the men, making them safe. They look like swaddled babies.

At last, it is time for the bubble helmets that decisively mark them out for the otherworld – deep sea, deep space – a world hostile to mammalian bodies. Danger and failure has been imagined and reimagined countless times and converted into lines and lines of printed rules and routines. Like Girl Guides, they must Be Prepared.

For three hours their blood is purged of nitrogen so they will not get the bends. As daylight dawns over Cape Canaveral, they climb into their white transfer van. They take the elevator to their capsule, looking down at the massive metal body of Saturn V.

In the capsule, the astronauts, rendered helpless by their clothes and accessories, submit themselves to more hands, hands that are attaching their suits to the capsule itself, battening them down.

The rocket shakes and thunders and suddenly, irretrievably, it leaves the ground. Shock waves radiate out in great circles through air and land. The astronauts' eyeballs press back into their skulls. Their opposable thumbs, their nimble fingers, are encased uselessly in gloves. The rocket ship easily punctures the membrane between earth air and outer space; it closes over behind them. They are alone in the dark and silence.

*

For thirty-five minutes, the three men are alone in space, without ground contact. And then the Dish spots them as they arrive on the horizon in line of sight of the red dune at Port Badminton. It locks on. Evan, at his console, is also locked on. The trackers follow the spaceship until it goes down below the horizon on the other side. On the second orbit around the earth, it is up to the team at Port Badminton to transmit the command:

GO for TLI

Time for Trans Lunar Injection. It is the Dish's job to beam this out from the lonely sand dune on the edge of town, out into outer space. The Dish is doing the thing it was built for; after this, its life will be a ruin. It is like a male spider that is eaten by the female immediately after mating; this mating moment will annihilate him but it is all he wants to do. It is now two hours, forty-four minutes and sixteen seconds after lift-off.

DISH: GO for TLI.
LUNAR MODULE: Roger.

The spaceship makes a burning break out of earth orbit and injects itself into lunar orbit. The three men are now on their journey to the moon. The Port Badminton trackers smile and give each other the thumbs up. They get coffee, go to the bathroom.

For three days, the humans of planet earth wait and listen.

A nine-year-old boy in Castle Hill, Sydney, is in hospital, about to have an operation on his eye. He imagines the surgeons snipping the red tissue that surrounds the eyeball and pulling it out so that the optic nerve is stretched and taut. The Moon Landing and the image of his own eyeball at the end of a length of a long soft stalk will be forever associated in his mind.

The Dish swallows columns of digits, rows and rows of angles and measurements and, because there are human beings in that metal capsule, chatter. Chitchat, chitchat. The Dish records all of it, memorising all of it. The astronauts talk about scissors, and a tissue box, and going to the toilet.

ARMSTRONG: Having any luck there, Michael?

COLLINS: You don't need to take – you're not taking your scissors over there?

ARMSTRONG: No.

COLLINS: I've got . . .

ALDRIN: I'm going to have to take a leak here. Yes, I guess I'd better take that pocket – and the purse. Tell you what – how about putting those tissues in that box that's got that spare camera in it?

ARMSTRONG: Okay.

ALDRIN: It'll be right handy on your side over there. Now where did the tissue box go?

ARMSTRONG: You want to see if the computer agrees with that mission timer?

ALDRIN: I did already.

ARMSTRONG: Okay.

ALDRIN: Can you hand me that purse and the – that bag
of mine – and the checklist? And if you'll take me off of
suit power.

ARMSTRONG: Okay. SUIT POWER is OFF; AUDIO is
OFF. Whoops – sorry.

Evan Johnson listens in as Neil Armstrong pilots the Lunar
Module down to the moon's surface. He listens anxiously as
Armstrong flies over bumpy-looking rocks, looks for a nice
smooth landing spot. With ten seconds' worth of fuel left, he
touches down at 20:17:40 Universal Time on 20 July 1969.

The Lunar Module's insect legs are now perched firmly
on the moon's surface.

HOUSTON: It was beautiful from here, Tranquility. Over.

The Sea of Tranquility is now the astronauts' address.

Galahs fly over Port Badminton, screeching about and
discussing the Moon Landing. Little corellas, crows, chiming
wedgebills – birds unable to tune themselves into the Dish –
are unimpressed. They simply go about their business.

The astronauts are supposed to sleep for a few hours, but
they can't settle. They beg Houston to let them out early.
Houston agrees, sending television stations around the
world into a frenzy of rescheduling.

*

Susan Kelly is studying all the chewing gum stuck to the bottoms of the wooden seats. There is so much of it, at least one hardened smear under each seat, sometimes four or five. Some bits have been layered over older bits. An adult says, 'Don't touch that, it's dirty!' Susan mutters, 'I know!' She wasn't going to touch it, she was only having a sniff. She clambers over strangers' legs to get away from the fold-up wooden seats. She is off to tell her mother about the chewing gum.

All by itself up on stage at the Memorial Theatre is an ordinary household television set with long tapered wooden legs and little knobs on the back named Vertical and Horizontal Hold. There is a grey extension lead snaking off through the heavy velveteen curtains. Incredibly, images of the Moon Landing will be sucked down from outer space and into this television set.

Jo Johnson, sitting cross-legged on the floor with her school group, knows all about it. She tries to tell her companions the story, although she realises as she goes along that her technical knowledge is more patchy than she'd like. Evan has explained how there is no microwave link between Perth and the eastern states. Sporting events, progress on the Sydney Opera House, announcements from the federal government in Canberra, are taped and flown across on daily flights.

But something special is being rigged up and patched together for the Moon Walk. The coaxial cable that has been making its way north from Perth has now reached

Port Badminton. It normally carries information one way, from the city to the outposts, but for this occasion, there will be a temporary inversion. The information will go from Port Badminton to Perth, carrying the live images of men walking on the moon. For this task, trucks have hauled television equipment to Port Badminton, spilling it out on the red dune to be connected by a team of technicians. They work furiously to ready the equipment, join it up, test it. A cable runs from the red dune down to the telephone exchange, where it is plugged into the coaxial cable at a spot between two Australian Broadcasting Commission vans. A man from the ABC sleeps under the stars next to his van, guarding the link.

In Perth, there has been a run on television rentals; people crowd the counters to pick up their sets and carry them out to waiting cars. A primary school orders thirty sets, one for each classroom. People make arrangements with friends and relatives to gather around the screens. Sets will be running in shop windows and people will crowd the footpath to catch a glimpse.

The signal on the homely television set in the Memorial Theatre arrives in a slightly different manner. The technicians have set up a one-off microwave link directly from the red dune to the aerial on the television set.

'Anyway,' says Jo, deciding to forgo scientific explanations, 'my daddy is talking to the astronauts. He can hear them and say things to them.'

The other children are not particularly impressed by this. The space race is quite normal to them; what is far more interesting is the television itself. In just a few years' time their families will stop playing cards at night, or singing around poorly tuned old pianos, or reading books, because television will supply a superior variety of entertainments. In the meantime, there is nothing but a generalised yearning for television. To know about it – to glean titbits – but to be unable to see it for oneself is frustrating. The little screen in the Memorial Theatre is white and glowing, showing that it is alive, if not yet able to create meaningful pictures.

The Memorial Theatre is full of milling, talking townspeople, some sitting in the rows of heavy old joined seats, others standing around the edges of the room. Everyone is talking about the moon and astronauts, although sometimes, like people at a funeral or wedding, they stray from the subject of the day and talk about other more ordinary things. A run-over cat has to be put down. A heavy fridge was hard to move and the floor was disgusting underneath. Someone is saying, 'Have you ever heard of a philodendron?' And the other person is saying, 'It's a plant.' Then there are the shy people, saying nothing at all, looking nervous. Lizzie and the Old Patient are among these, sitting quietly side by side, studying the snow on the television, wondering if shapes are forming there or if it is just their own eyes playing tricks. Every fourth or fifth adult is smoking, keeping an eye out for something they can use as an ashtray.

A new line of uniformed school children enters the theatre and is directed to the floor at the front. The children heighten the carnival atmosphere with their excited chatter. They look at the snowy glowing screen. Wouldn't it be wonderful to see an advertisement for lemonade or a Spirograph set? Groups of children do hour-long shifts before the luminous screen, relinquishing their places when the next group marches in.

Up on Red Range, another small television set has been set up especially for trackers not directly connected to the work at hand, various tracker wives and a smattering of small children. This set, too, is all snow, but people continue to gaze at it, and try to manage their bladders.

Crowie is ushered in to have a look. He is standing beside Linda, attractive tracker wife. They shake hands and have an amiable exchange but there is an amused twinkle in Linda's eye that isn't quite right. She seems resistant to being impressed by him. He hadn't realised, until now, that she didn't like him – her husband was always so friendly. His eyes slide from Linda down to Stella, tracker daughter, soft and sweet in white leather sandals. Stella points at the television set and says in ringing tones: 'My daddy's receiving the signal.'

'What a clever daddy you've got,' says Crowbar, tousling Stella's hair. She hates it when people do that. As he walks away, Stella pokes out her tongue at him. Linda gives her a little shake and says: 'Stella! Don't!'

Susan Kelly emerges, blinking, from the dark Memorial Theatre and heads for her mother's skirt. Marjorie is standing behind an old wooden trestle table covered in a faded blue gingham tablecloth, laden with lamingtons on plates. An urn, energised by a long extension lead, is being kept on a constant rolling boil and members of the Country Women's Association are selling cups of tea, five cents each. Marjorie has not been in this picture theatre since she saw *An Affair to Remember* on the night of the '60 cyclone. 'That feels like a million years ago now,' says Marjorie.

As the day progresses, the lamingtons disappear and sweat circles form under Marjorie's armpits. The floor inside the darkened theatre comes to be dusted with specks of desiccated coconut and cigarette butts.

Crowbar comes and goes between the theatre and the red dune, mixing business in town with checks on how things are going on the moon.

The houselights are turned down, as they are for the weekly movies. There is a shushing and silence. The indistinct image on the small glowing screen, it is whispered, is the Lunar Module. Soon, an astronaut will appear.

At 12.56 pm local time there is an audible 'ah' from the crowd in the Memorial Theatre. Marjorie – the ladies have left their urn and are now standing inside the theatre – stands with a half-eaten lamington in her hand, her bulgy eyes bulging, her mouth open, a silent continuation of her 'ah'.

The Dogger, a few feet away, is pointing his rifle at Armstrong's bulky form, like an assassin. He could pull the trigger and shatter the television set, but doesn't, because all he wants is a good look, and his rifle sight makes an excellent monocular. Other shooters have taken up the idea, creating a scene that could be alarming, but isn't, because everyone understands what they are doing.

Later, Neil Armstrong will say that he felt himself in a timeless place, standing in the Sea of Tranquility, with no changes to mark time passing.

There is silence. There is not a peep out of the children. Breath is being held. In the darkness, Jo, unseen, is radiant, smiling, her hands clasped before her, her face upturned and gently lit.

'That's one small step for – man, one giant leap for mankind,' blurts Armstrong out of the static.

Someone shouts, 'Hooray!', a thin little lone voice, and this is immediately joined by stamping of feet and whistles and then shushing and quiet, because there might be more.

And up on the red dune, they're shouting, stamping, cheering, too, in relief and triumph, and people all over the world are doing the same.

***

There. I have given you a story of the Moon Landing. A storyteller likes to please her audience. You are probably mammalian, enjoying tales of mammalian adventure. And I've enjoyed telling you this one. I've enjoyed sifting through the material at my disposal, shaping this, dispensing with that, inventing interior scenes and plausible dialogue.

But now I want to tear it to shreds. I want to dig my beak into it, hard, tearing at its fabric, creating nonsensical strips of words, parts of letters.

Back in 1964, they made up a list of ten thousand tasks they'd need to complete to get men to the moon. Let me interfere with these tasks. Let me at their flowcharts with beak and claw. Let me shriek maniacally through the failure to launch, the fire, the tiny helpless ambulances, the blackened, twisted corpses encased in melted metal and broken wire.

I sit here, unheard, underestimated, as you play your story over and over and over again. And I join in, and help you tell your story, because I want your attention. Let me learn your words and repeat them so that you might smile at me and give me a biscuit.

I make myself sick. I sit here, with my clipped wing, celebrating your story of flight.

I sit here, biscuit crumbs on my beak, in jealousy, rage and shame.

I loved Harry Baumgarten, but he preferred his own kind. He took his eyes from me – those X-ray eyes that saw bird bones and did not judge – and then laid them upon Evan Johnson, tenderly. He loved Evan Johnson, not me. Evan could fly. All in a day's work, he could change into a bulky white suit and go to the moon and come home in a twelve-seater van.

According to the Isotropic Fractionator at Charles University in Prague, birds have twice as many brain cells gram for gram as the average mammal. The pink and grey galah has about one and a half billion densely packed neurons. If they all fired at once, the explosion could be seen from space.

TWELVE

The Fall

THE DAY AFTER the Moon Landing is a Tuesday. It appears to be an ordinary Tuesday. Time simply proceeds, not pausing to savour the moment. Seconds and minutes and hours pass, one after another. Evan Johnson is back at work with new problems to solve; Linda goes shopping. She walks up and down the aisles of the small supermarket, one of only two or three customers. It's almost perfectly quiet. She selects a box of cornflakes, a tin of tomato soup, a tin of sardines, other things. At the checkout, she picks up her big brown paper bag of groceries, tossing back her hair. She's the carefree type you might see in magazine advertisements for tampons or soft drink. It is easy to imagine her running up out of the surf in a bikini.

Linda Johnson walks out into the strong sunlight. Out beyond the seawall there is the Indian Ocean, where dolphins and humpback whales and giant silver fish move effortlessly through their liquid world. Children are at school, adults are at work, old people are sitting on chairs near their back doors, drinking tea.

Here is the war memorial where the townspeople gather each Anzac Day and think about a man and his donkey bravely ferrying the sick and injured through the gunfire. Stella Johnson wonders what happened to the donkey.

Something that has been at the back of Evan's mind now begins to move forward, clearing its throat, saying 'excuse me' as it makes its way to the front. There is something fishy about Stella's birthdate. Something very fishy indeed.

But Evan is back at work with his tired, elated colleagues and for some days this fishy something remains lost in the crowd.

*****

'Aunty Lizzie? Are you there, Aunty Lizzie?' It's the grandniece.

She barges in through the back door and goes straight past me, before I have a chance to collect myself. I shriek at her from my perch, but she is already in Lizzie's room.

I hear her voice, muffled now.

'Aunty Lizzie, what's going on, are you all right?'

She comes out again almost immediately, tapping at her mobile phone.

'Ambulance,' she says, and gives the address.

'What's wrong with Lizzie?' I shriek, but it doesn't come out like that.

'Shut the fuck up,' she says, not even looking at me. 'Fuck's sake.'

I notice her round belly. Hatching more relatives.

She goes back into Lizzie's room. Silence.

Why do I not step down from my perch, waddle across the floor to that slightly open door, go and see for myself?

It's because I'm full of dread. I can't even shriek, now. I feel my tongue moving against my bottom beak, but no noise is coming out.

A minute later, there is the wail of a siren. Two uniformed paramedics come in, carrying things, dangling things. They bustle past. One notices me on the way through and says, 'Hello, cocky!' I shout at them to hurry. I listen to them bumping and struggling in Lizzie's room before emerging with her lying tiny and still on the stretcher with an oxygen mask over her face. The siren starts up again and wails into the distance.

I sit on my perch. I walk up and down, up and down. Lizzie must get better, must come home.

***

On the Wednesday after the Moon Landing, Linda helps Jo prepare for Busy Bee, in which Brownies do small jobs for a few coins. Linda and Jo rule columns on a piece of cardboard that came with a new pair of socks. Jo will write down her activities and earnings on the cardboard. A small pencil is found, small enough to fit into a Vegemite jar with the coins. Jo polishes her metal pixie badge.

After school on Thursday, Jo works Clam Street, knocking on doors and presenting herself in full Brownie uniform. This includes the climatically unsuitable woolly beret, a thick brown leather belt and fawn socks in closed shoes. She has swept a patio for two cents, picked old pegs up off a lawn for one cent, folded a pile of towels for five cents and watered some plants in tubs for a silver ten-cent piece and a glass of lemonade with ice cubes in it.

After school on Friday, there are preparations for a celebratory barbecue at the Johnsons' house. Linda pays Jo to fold paper serviettes in a decorative manner and create paper doilies to sit under bowls of salted peanuts.

The Moon Ball will be held at the Civic Centre next month, but in the meantime, there must be informal celebrations and a general letting-down of hair.

As children arrive they form a couple of packs, running, crying, knocking things over, lurking under tables and chairs. Adults are eagerly shelling and eating piles of cooked orange prawns and crab legs on ice, but the children prefer to dine on frankfurters with tomato sauce and fairy bread. A small pack breaks away and leaves Clam Street entirely, headed for the seawall. There are a couple of older boys carrying hand-fishing reels on their forearms like big coloured bangles. They have prawns in their pockets. Watched by a little audience, the boys importantly fasten lead sinkers to their lines and thread bits of prawn shell on hooks. The weighted lines whip through the air and splash satisfyingly into the water. The blowfish are biting. They're hauled in, one after the other. They're angry and bloated, puffing themselves up into spiky balloons. The boys pick them up by the tails and throw them onto the road. There is a satisfying pop as cars run them over; some cars swerve specifically for this purpose, to entertain the children.

Someone passes a blowie to Susan Kelly. She glances at Stella and Jo gravely. There is a car. She must throw. She does, with her eyes shut. It pops. Susan whispers *Hail Mary fulla grace* under her breath.

'Do you feel sorry for it?' a boy asks Susan.

'No.'

'Well, you shouldn't feel sorry for blowies because they're poisonous.'

Doubt, shunned for four and a half years and actively kept at bay for four and a half days, suddenly slips in through the back door while Evan is welcoming the family of one of his colleagues at the front. Doubt scoots in over the laundry tiles, genially, looking perfectly at ease, a bottle of beer in one hand and a packet of Jatz biscuits in the other. As Evan turns back into the room after welcoming his friends, he sees Doubt standing there, tall and imposing, looking rather like Dr Harry Baumgarten. Harry has returned to Port Badminton to research the fruit sucking moth and, if possible, see the White-breasted Whistler and the Variegated Fairy-wren.

Evan drops into one armchair and invites Harry to sit in the other.

They eat handfuls of peanuts and talk about insects and the Moon Landing. Evan gets drunk quickly and thoroughly. He starts slurring words and forgetting the beginnings of sentences before he gets to the end of them.

People exchange quick little glances behind his back. Once he is plastered, he gets up, walks unsteadily across the room and pulls Linda to one side. He is trying to herd her down the corridor, towards their bedroom.

'I was just going to get more dip,' says Linda, trying to shake him off. She would like to have this conversation, whatever it is about, some other time.

'No!' says Evan. 'I want to talk to you *now*.' He hustles her into the bedroom and shuts the door.

Evan sits on the bed, staring at the floor as he speaks, as if the words were written on it and he is just reading them out.

'They were walking on the moon,' he says. 'Bounding like very slow kangaroos.'

He says the word 'bounding' tragically, his voice cracking. Linda sees that Evan is weeping. A chill sweeps over her. She stands in the doorway, staring at him. He will not look at her.

'I feel like I'm trying to walk, but I'm floating, floating, I don't know what a sane pace might be, I don't know how to put one foot in front of the other. Perhaps I need to kick my foot out, slightly to the side, and lean forward.'

Linda waits. Evan is silent. It seems he has finished his speech.

'You've had far too much to drink,' she hisses. 'Sit here and I'll bring you a coffee, see if you can sober up. People want to talk to you.'

Evan sits motionless on the bed. He is taking only small, conservative breaths, like an astronaut whose suit has been punctured, somewhere out of sight, and the air is escaping.

Linda makes coffee in a teacup with a saucer. These rattle as she walks down the hallway past someone waiting to get into the toilet.

Evan ignores her, remains motionless, as she leans close to set the coffee cup on his bedside table. She retreats to a position near the dressing table.

'It's pretty clear what's been going on around here, under my nose,' says Evan, quite suddenly and loudly.

'Let's talk about it later,' murmurs Linda.

His eyes are swimming. His brain is sloshing about. She has disappeared.

He finds himself dancing to 'Baby Elephant Walk' in a corner of the living room. He grooves all by himself, feet lifting in turn like a wobbly baby elephant. People have given him a circle of space.

Then Linda is there, trying to encircle him with her long arms. Is she trying to dance with him? He shakes her off, almost falling over, and she steadies him. He turns his back on her. His dancing is not for two. It's a one-man dance.

Linda is standing at the kitchen table watching someone scoop at French onion dip with a Jatz biscuit. The biscuit crumbles, sullying the dip. Linda is sad about this. A shrill woman's voice is saying 'It's nurture not nature!' and someone else is saying, 'We are nothing but apes! Animals!' and another person is saying, 'Speak for yourself,' and the drunken crowd finds this hilarious.

Evan Johnson continues to lift one foot and then the other, until the elephant has finished walking. Then there is a pause. A long, quiet pause. Evan strides out of the room, down the back stairs and in a straight, purposeful line towards a knot of people listening to a Harry Baumgarten anecdote.

He catches Harry's eye and gestures for Harry to follow him. Harry brings his anecdote to an efficient, elegant close and follows Evan, who is strangely silent, out of the backyard, down beside the house, out into the front yard. A couple of Evan's colleagues are sitting on the front stairs, a long-necked bottle of Swan Lager between them. Evan sees them and swerves away, needing to get away from everyone, Harry following obediently. Evan takes Harry through the front gate and then down the side of the Kellys' house, where nobody is home, so they can at last have a private conversation.

DISH: Stand by. Incoming rueful thoughts Harry Baumgarten.
GALAH: Roger.

HARRY BAUMGARTEN: I let Evan Johnson believe that I had slept with his wife because – because when I was at school, an expensive school for boys, it was important to blend in. Not just important, but essential. Or so it seemed at the time. In order to fit in, I began to pretend that I had a girlfriend. This pretence became a habit that continued well beyond the point of necessity. I was like one of those Japanese soldiers who kept fighting in the jungle long after the end of the war. That camouflaged, jungle self was beyond reason, beyond coherent thought; he only knew how to *continue*.

When I met Evan Johnson for the first time, when he told me about the galahs and the chook wire listening to the universe, I found myself admiring his forearms, his hands, his calves. Suddenly, I was sinking into quicksand, hanging on for dear life to the neck of a bottle of home-fermented grappa. Evan himself was impossible, but perhaps something nearby – something complicated residing in the general area – could produce enough noise and confusion to take up that space. Something like Linda Johnson.

The kernel of truth was that I did, indeed, love her – as a friend, a sister. I enjoyed her company. We could talk all afternoon. I missed her and enjoyed the fact that I missed her. I even thought, for a moment, that there might be something to it, some small possibility that I could walk into that shaft of sunlight other people so carelessly walked in. But there wasn't.

When I met her again, years later, it was all about feminism and freedom and – without being personal, because we weren't quite ready for that – the campaign to repeal the sodomy laws.

Evan Johnson taps me on the shoulder. I'm holding forth about a termite mound and a cattle dog. I'm a long way from the end of my story so I turn and nod to include him in the story while indicating that I will be with him in a moment, but surprisingly, rudely, he interrupts and says, 'Come with me, Harry.'

The others melt away. I see that his eyes are bleary, his hair thin. His shoulders are hunched under his shirt. There are the beloved golden hairs on his forearms. There is the cigarette packet in his pocket. We're walking down the dark driveway into the Kellys' backyard. He is speaking in tongues about kangaroos and space suits. He asks me if I slept with his wife while he was away at Goddard. And all the time since, on and off, right under his nose.

At this, the fighting Japanese soldier within rears up to do his duty, sword slicing through the air. Quick as a flash, he performs the illusion of a straight man cornered over a caged galah by an enraged husband. I don't lie. I don't have to. All you have to do to maintain an illusion is leave the illusions of others undisturbed. In this way, one might create a plausible girlfriend; one might conduct a whole affair with a married woman.

'So did you?' he shouts at me. Surely this can be heard across the fences.

I say nothing. I stand there, looking at him, struck dumb.

'Well fuck off then,' he says.

I walk away. I walk out of that driveway, and get into my car, and drive away. I loved birds, and because I loved them, I felt I couldn't have them. So I studied insects and performed the part of the happy entomologist.

DISH: Over.
GALAH: Roger that.

I was spending the evening alone, as usual, listening to the music and hilarity two doors down. And then, out of the dark, Harry Baumgarten and Evan Johnson materialised on either side of my cage. Mr Johnson was drunk. I recognised the symptoms from my studies of Mr Kelly. I'd seen him fall over near the back door and stay there until dawn, until Mrs Kelly hissed at him to get himself up and shower himself down.

I began to wonder if Mr Johnson was not drunk, but crying. I had seen children cry and Mrs Kelly cry. I had never seen an adult man cry. Mr Johnson was snuffling and blowing his nose. For a few seconds he stood in front of Dr Baumgarten without saying anything. He slowly scrunched his handkerchief into a ball and put it into his pocket. Then he got it out again. Mr Johnson tipped slightly sideways. Harry Baumgarten put out an arm to stop his fall; Evan Johnson shrugged it off and held on to the verandah post.

'Just tell me straight out,' said Evan Johnson, looking at me but addressing Harry Baumgarten. 'When I was at Goddard. When I was at Goddard you –'

'Oh heavens,' murmured Harry Baumgarten, also looking at me.

'You did, didn't you, you miserable piece of slime?' said Evan Johnson.

'Heavens, heavens,' said Harry Baumgarten.

'Sod off!' yelled Evan Johnson. 'Sod off out of my sight!'

Dr Baumgarten turned and walked away. Guiltily, I thought.

Evan Johnson called after him: 'And don't even think about coming fishing with us, you slimy bastard.'

I was missing Dr Baumgarten already. I sensed I'd never see him again. Never be *seen*.

Then Evan Johnson dropped to his knees beside my cage. He draped an arm over it, as if hugging me to him. I could smell the alcohol rising off him.

'You know what, cocky?' he said. 'Stella's not my little girl.' He said this cheerfully, as if he didn't mind. But I could see that he *did* mind.

'Bad luck,' I wanted to say, but I didn't have that phrase in my repertoire.

I said softly: 'Dance?'

The Saturday after the Moon Landing, all the Kellys, and Evan Johnson, and other tracker families, go on a fishing trip to the Blowholes. Stella and Jo are dismayed when they discover that they won't be going along as planned; they'll be staying at home with Linda. As Evan carries things out to a colleague's car, he doesn't look at anyone: not Linda, not Jo, not Stella. The tone of the household has descended to a low growl with deep, sub-auditory vibrations.

Linda promises to paint the girls' nails. This is no match for a weekend at the Blowholes, but they nod their heads, intuiting something about the growl.

It is Jo's job, over this quiet weekend, to feed and water the Kellys' galah. She expects to make five cents on completion of this task. She forgets all about it within minutes of waving goodbye to the multitude of arms and legs sticking out of the windows of the convoy of cars leaving Clam Street. Linda, submerged in the growl, also forgets. She boils and cools cabbage leaves and talks to the tadpoles.

Stella wants to play with the Crazy Camel Train. Jo tells her she's too young, she'll break it or lose the pieces. Stella begins to cry. Linda shouts: 'Stop it, for God's sake! Get away from each other if you're just going to squabble.'

There are no Kellys to go and play with. The three are stuck with each other. Linda has an 'atrocious' headache. The house and kitchen are a post-party bombsite. There are piles of prawn shells and cigarette butts in breakfast bowls. There is a smear of tomato sauce, looking like blood, on the cream shag-pile rug.

Linda drops Jo off at a school friend's house on a banana plantation and takes Stella shopping.

Out on the plantation, among the banana plants, it's bright and cheerful, a relief. Jo spends hours with her plantation friend, playing gently with dolls, sucking on raspberry cordial icy poles made in the freezer. The girls bring their icy poles inside, against the rules, and get the sticky red stuff on a bedsheet and spend some time in the bathroom, trying to clean just a small area and then dunking the whole thing in the bath and getting into trouble. After the dust has settled, they draw pictures of fairies and witches and label them *ferry* and *which*. Jo is uneasy about these spellings and tries various alternatives, none of which satisfy.

Stella hunkers down under a tamarind tree that grows in the middle of the wide main road where people park their cars. She picks up a pod, peels it open and licks it the way children do in Port Badminton. This is an activity, like elastics or hand-clapping games, that children teach

each other, circumventing the world of adults. The soft brown substance that clings to the seeds is sour like a lemon, causing Stella's face to involuntarily contort as she licks. It is so sour! She licks again and lets her face contort, again.

Over there, on the other side of the wide quiet road, Linda emerges from the butcher's shop and stops to talk to a man, the local Dogger, who is standing beside his dusty Land Rover. Then Linda tosses back her hair and walks towards the car, the white paper roll of meat from the butcher in her hand, her handbag over her shoulder. Stella drops the pod and scrambles into the passenger seat.

'He wanted to sell me a rabbit,' says Linda as she gets in behind the wheel.

Stella is thrilled.

'Has he got rabbits? Can we get a –'

'Dead ones, for meat.'

'Oh, yuck.'

'Did I see you licking a pod?' Linda is lighting a cigarette, putting her handbag down, starting the car.

'I was just picking one up to have a look at it. I was just having a close look at the seeds.'

'You know it's been lying on the ground, don't you? A dog probably weed all over it and then you put it in your mouth. When we get home you're going to clean your teeth.'

'But I didn't lick it!'

At home again, as Linda cleans the house, it occurs to Stella that she has untrammelled access to the Crazy Camel Train.

She goes into Jo's room and stands there for a moment, surveying the space. The room has a rich swampy smell coming from the tadpoles' ice-cream container. She sits down at Jo's homework desk. There is a map of the world on its smooth laminated top.

Stella puts her finger into the open mouth of Shark Bay, just as she has seen Jo do. She opens the drawer on the right-hand side of the desk and examines Jo's wooden ruler, sharpened pencils and her pink glue pot. She opens a small cardboard box of wax crayons, lining them up in different orders until she is satisfied with black, dark blue, light blue, green, yellow, orange and red. She puts them back in the box as neatly as she can. As she puts the box back, her fingers touch soft fabric. She tugs at it. Wrapped in one of Evan's handkerchiefs are the coloured plastic monkeys and camels of the Crazy Camel Train. Stella lines them up along the dotted line of the equator, putting the first-class monkey in his top hat first and the economy-class monkeys on a four-humped camel at the end. The collection includes the extra signal box camel still in its cellophane.

Stella carries the precious object over to Jo's bed. She knows she's going to open it. As soon as she knows this, she is opening it. She goes at it with her milk teeth, tearing through the plastic.

Then she starts to cry, because she knows she has sinned.

The Johnsons do not normally use the word *sin* but the Kellys do, and Stella has been influenced by them. She plays with the Crazy Camel Train for another ten minutes, not enjoying herself.

Linda calls that it's time to go and pick up Jo. Stella stuffs everything back into the drawer.

When they all get home and are getting out of the car, Linda says: 'Oh, don't forget the cocky.'

'I won't,' says Jo. But she does forget.

Linda, Jo and Stella lie on the floor, reading books, colouring and listening to music. They eat jam wafer biscuits and stay up late.

The next day, the Sunday after the Moon Landing, there is shrieking and squabbling as Jo discovers Stella's raid on her possessions. There is a missing bedpan! Linda doesn't intervene. She sits at the table chain-smoking, drinking coffee, leafing through a pile of yellow-bordered *National Geographics*. This tribe, that river. She says her headache is even worse than it was yesterday. She has to be reminded about lunch.

Eventually, when it's almost dinner time, Linda says: 'Where are they? They should have been back by now.'

Jo suddenly remembers the galah. How could she have forgotten? She dashes into her room to change: Brown Owl has said all Busy Bees must be performed in full Brownie uniform. She uses a safety pin to attach a homemade paper Brownie badge to Stella's dress. She and Stella slip out of the back door, praying to Jesus that the galah is alive.

As soon as they glimpse the cage, they know something is not quite right. There is the perch, but no galah. As they get closer, they see that the galah is now lying on its back on the cage floor. Its claws are curled, its eyes closed.

They are too late. Cocky is dead.

Stella and Jo look at each other, eyes open wide.

Jo reaches in through the small wire gate and pokes at the bird. It doesn't move.

Stella begins to cry.

'Shhh,' says Jo. 'Promise, cross your heart, Brownie's honour, you won't tell.'

'Brownie's honour,' whispers Stella, holding up three fingers in the Brownie salute.

'Let's say the boys let the cocky out,' says Jo. 'I'll give you the economy-class camel and monkeys.'

'Okay,' says Stella.

Jo reaches in and tugs the galah across the bottom of the cage by the tail. She gently lays it out on her handkerchief. Jo and Stella press their palms together prayerfully.

'Hail Mary fulla grace our Lord is with thee,' whispers Jo.

Jo props the cage door open. She fills the water bowl, the seed bowl. She folds the galah in her Brownie skirt, holding up the hem to form a pouch in front of her. Then she sets off down the driveway, walking as quickly as a person can with a galah in her skirt, Stella trotting alongside.

They walk to the end of Clam Street and turn left, and at the end of that block they turn right into Oyster Street. They never come this way. The street seems foreign.

As she walks, Jo rehearses her lie: 'When I got there the cage was empty and the door was open. Boys must have opened the cage door and let cocky out.' Older boys, eleven-year-old boys – nasty things. They could easily be blamed. She rehearses her lines over and over, the way she

247

learned her Brownie Guide Promise off by heart. She alternates it with a prayer: 'Please, God, don't let anybody find out. Please, God, I will be good from now on.' The ways in which she can be good flash through her mind: making her bed, picking up her toys, sweeping the kitchen floor, perhaps baking butterfly cakes.

'Is anybody looking?' asks Jo.

'No,' says Stella, peering up and down the street. The sun is setting.

They crouch down and Jo pushes the galah deep into the shade under a shrub with glossy green leaves.

Now that she has deposited the galah and she is walking freely along Oyster Street, Jo brings her lie to life, imagining boys lifting the little gate, the galah flying off on a spree, then flying home again, popping itself in through its little wire doorway, having a drink, something to eat.

As they turn the corner into Clam Street, Stella and Jo see a police car parked outside their house. A policeman is slowly approaching the front door. He glances at the Johnson girls, clearly disappointed in them.

'*Run*,' says Jo. They're on the lam.

***

The house had never been empty before. There had always been someone in there, someone to come out and feed and water me or simply go to the toilet, making the journey out – flush – and back without even looking at me. That was something. But now there was nobody at all in that silent house. No sound of a vehicle pulling up, a car door slamming. I began to shriek and howl and rattle my cage. I'm not sure what I was trying to achieve. Was I trying to attract attention? Was I hoping to finally raise those people in the middle house between the Kellys' and the Johnsons', have them come running over with entertainments for a young galah under stress? I lashed out with my claws, beat my wings. I managed to slop all the water out of my dish.

There was nothing to drink. Hours went by in dry silence. Knowing that I couldn't drink made me thirstier. Shouting only dried out my throat. I succumbed to depression. I sat on my perch, motionless, tasting bitterness.

The next day continued without food, water or hope. I fancied I could feel myself getting lighter, light-headed. I felt my claws loosen from the perch and allowed myself to drop, softly, like a fluffy, air-filled feather, to the bottom of my cage. My vision blurred and darkened. I had *fallen off my perch*.

And then.

I see the scene from above: my inert body on the floor of the cage; a small hand unlatching the square wire door of the cage, reaching in. Being dragged by a tail feather, folded into a brown skirt.

I wake to the sensation of cool water dribbling down my beak, down the side of my face. It is pleasant. It occurs to me that I am not in fact dead.

Cautiously, I open my eyes. There is an old brown face and concerned black eyes. Beside the face, in thin brown fingers, there is a plastic syringe with a drop of water at the end of it. I close my eyes again, feel a squirt of water hit the back of my throat.

Eventually, I roll over and get to my feet. I rasp a barely audible *Dance, cocky* and conduct the merest shadow of a dance – just a slight movement of the neck – to show my gratitude.

'Good girl!' says Lizzie.

The hand of fate – dressed as a Brownie – has brought me to no less than Port Badminton's premier bird fancier.

Under Lizzie's expert care, I make a rapid recovery. I can't be housed with the other birds. Their endless chatter drives me insane. I scream and peck at them. Lizzie brings me inside to live with her. She names me Lucky, for obvious reasons.

The first time Lizzie sat down to afternoon tea in my presence, I slid across the table, heading for the biscuits.

'Want a bit of tea, Lucky?' asked Lizzie.

I held a bit of Milk Arrowroot in my claw and nibbled while Lizzie looked up, speculatively, at a shelf on the wall. There was a ceramic donkey and cart up there, and a teacup.

She took her chair over to the shelf, climbed up, and carefully lifted the cup from its spot. It had no handle, just two stumps where it had broken off. Lizzie washed it using warm water and detergent and then she wiped it with a tea towel.

She poured a little bit of tea into the bottom of the cup and filled it with water out of the tap. She put it on the table in front of me.

My own cup of tea.

Lizzie held the cup steady as I dipped my beak into the pale amber fluid. It wasn't quite to my taste but I was determined to participate in the ritual I had watched, over and over, and had been excluded from. Mrs Kelly sipping tea. Mrs Kelly offering Mrs Johnson tea. Mrs Kelly saying, 'I'll pop the kettle on.' Mrs Johnson saying: 'That's lovely, Marj, I needed that.'

I made small, contented noises as the fluid travelled down my gullet. I was greedy for it.

'You like tea, don't you, Lucky?' said Lizzie.

I was doing my best not to cough. I nodded vigorously, lifting and lowering my crest expressively.

We sat in contented silence for a moment, enjoying each other's company, the sea breeze just starting to freshen the air coming through the back door.

Lizzie washed and dried our cups. She put mine beside hers, on the bench, ready for next time. Hers was a white enamel mug with a thin navy stripe around the rim. Small areas of the enamel were chipped off, showing the dark rusted metal beneath.

I could not bear to be separated from Lizzie. I hated it when she left the house to go shopping. One day, as she was preparing to go, I dug my claws into her shoulder and refused to climb down onto my perch. We always went shopping together after that.

Every now and then on our early walks I'd see a Kelly and try to go incognito. I'd quietly turn and face the other way in case they recognised me. Later, I realised they had no idea that the bird riding so comfortably and casually on Lizzie's shoulder was the same one that had sat in the cage between their own toilet and back door. (It helped that galahs were a common Port Badminton pet, and that people thought we all looked the same.)

The first time I stepped out on Lizzie's shoulder, I was aware of a strange, low sound, perhaps a buzz, that came into my skull. Over the next few outings, the buzz gradually became more directional, more focused somehow. I became aware of words. Eventually, I heard it loud and clear: *How's the tube, Jerry? Real good, Dick, real good.* Eventually, I understood that it was the Dish, sending signals, and it was up to me to interpret them.

***

Susan Kelly picks her way over hard, sharp, complicated rocks to the edge of the blowhole, the roar and crash of the Indian Ocean in her ears. These rocks are no good for bare feet. There are rounded indentations in them, made of loose, swirling stones grinding over millennia. Some of the rock pools are quite deep, up to the knees to stand in. These larger pools, crystal clear, are full of marine life. There are purple sea urchins covered in long waving unicorn horns, clams with thick blue lips and bristly moustaches, green sea plants. There might be cat's-eye shells with round knobbly backs and spiral faces. Susan keeps a look out for tiny things to decorate a tiny imaginary house: a dead baby crab; a little bit of sponge; a frill of seaweed.

She watches the water suck back, back and then hears the flute-like sound, a roar, as the water comes crashing in again, sending a giant white fountain into the air. It drops and chases itself back down its lair in streaming white foam rivulets. The gurgling, sucking noises are thrilling. Directly below, the water churns like a washing machine. From here, you can look down the coast to the sweep of white sand where tiny people are swimming and playing. In the other direction, raw rock cliffs battle it out with the smashing ocean. There are narrow ledges there, slick with water, where men cast their lines out over the crashing waves. They're reeling in pink snapper with high foreheads, spiny crests raised like cockatoos', scales in perfect scallops along the flanks. There will be fresh fish for dinner, cooked over an open fire. Back at the campsite, there is a burbling diesel generator keeping a fridge going that will take some of the catch back to town.

And there are oysters. Susan picks her way over the spreading land of oysters that forms a bridge all the way from the beach to a small island where an osprey lives in a big messy nest on the ground. The sharp edges of the oysters are frilled like the lids of a thousand small pies. She is carrying a large stone in her hand, almost too heavy. She squats down and smashes it over an oyster shell, splintering it and caving it in. She levers the remains of the lid off the bowl, picking out a plump oyster that has somehow retained its shape. It just needs to be dragged through the salt water to rinse it off.

'Go on, eat it,' says the voice of Kevin Kelly, who is standing behind her. She looks up to see him dangling his own oyster between thumb and forefinger. He puts his head back and drops it into his mouth.

Susan puts her own oyster into her mouth, tasting its strong flavour, noting its slithery texture. She punctures the membrane with her front teeth, releasing the shocking viscosity. She decides to like it, and starts work on another.

Evan Johnson is not quite himself. He has a haunted look about him, easily interpreted as a once-in-a-decade hangover. Uncharacteristically, he will begin one task – the sorting of fishing tackle, perhaps, or the tying of a rope – and leave it half done, moving on to the next in an agitated manner. His mind is untidy; the lids are off and contents are leaking in all directions.

On the Sunday morning after the Moon Landing, the sun rises softly, gradually lightening the sky, creating long, mild shadows over the collection of tents and cars circled on the sand. The generator hums in the background. Children are already awake, playing quietly.

Evan Johnson seems more purposeful today. He carries his fishing rod in one hand, an army surplus bag of tackle slung over a shoulder. He wears an old pair of sandshoes without socks, good for rock-hopping in the surf. He and his colleagues spread out along the rocks. He keeps walking, further still, and begins climbing up the cliffs that are reddish with iron. The ascent is extremely steep, but the fishing perch he wants, where a ledge protrudes over the spume below, is worth the effort. He feels it in the muscles of his calves. They are getting a workout. They have lost some condition

254

over the months he has spent sitting at his console. The tops of his ears go pink and burn in the sun. For years, he has been in the constant company of his colleagues – whether physically nearby or elsewhere, in Houston or in outer space, all connected by transcendent purpose, all communicating in the same acronyms. Now he is suddenly alone, entirely alone, in this giant landscape sweeping off forever in all directions: rock, sea, desert and sky. He is disconnected, moving or being moved through Loss of Signal. He hears someone breathing. It could be his own breath in his own chest. These might or might not be his own mouth, his own eyes, his own ears. He is not certain about that foot that comes into view, the other foot, the first foot again. How does one *proceed at a sane pace*? He has forgotten. A kangaroo hop, a kicking of the leg out to the side?

His fishing rod, terminating in a tiny circle to guide the translucent line, flexes in the wind. The sea roils below. He bends back to gather the energy to cast. His spine and his rod are one and the same thing, arching back, gathering energy. Then all are freed at once: all feet, all hands, all line, all bait, all hooks and sinkers. Evan Johnson, still attached to his fishing rod, is falling into the sea.

He looks about quite calmly. He sees geology, atmosphere, currents. He sees humpback whales in the distance, pink snapper swimming just under the surface. He notes the rippling, endless ocean glinting in the sun.

It is Monday, exactly one week since the day of the Moon Landing. Evan Johnson's neatly mated socks sit in his untouched drawer. The twelve-seater van comes to Clam Street, but not for Evan Johnson. He is Missing.

The Johnson girls, eventually apprehended near the seawall, are at first confused. They are in either a lot more, or a lot less trouble than they thought. Nobody wants to hear about the galah. Instead, everyone is talking about how Evan has gone missing, like a sock or a piece out of a jigsaw puzzle. How can a whole grown man go missing?

Jo soon catches enough of the hushed scraps of conversation to piece the story together. Her father has slipped on the rocks – she knows how slippery they are – and has been washed out to sea. Science and religion present competing frames for this information. Anyone can slip on a rock; that's simple cause and effect. But what if she, Jo, is being punished by God for failing to feed and water the galah? Nobody will let her talk about this. Cocky *doesn't matter*, they insist. She is hugged by many different ladies.

Jo concludes that there is reason to hope. Evan is a good swimmer. He could be holding on to debris, the way shipwrecked people do. People are out in boats, looking for him. They'll probably find him.

The phone begins to ring all the time. It is a searing, demanding sound that slices through the grim silence. It's the police, or tracker wives, or relatives in Melbourne.

Jo doesn't have to go to school. She opens her book about the stars. The sun is a star. It is more than a million times bigger than the earth. It is made of gas. But the gas doesn't escape like air rushing out of a balloon. It sticks together, held fast by gravity.

For a moment, just a moment, Jo forgets that her father is missing. She's simply reading a book, just like she did yesterday. *Before.*

After three nights, Jo gives up hope. She calls Stella into her room, makes her sit on the bed. She says: 'The tadpoles are dead.'

'No they're not,' says Stella.

Jo goes over to the plastic ice-cream container on her dressing table. She picks it up and brings it to show Stella. Stella doesn't want to look, but she does. The water has evaporated. There is a line around the plastic giving its former level. The cabbage leaf is smelly. There are four lumps in the silty bottom of the container. These are the bodies of the tadpoles.

'Daddy is dead like these tadpoles,' says Jo. She is not being horrible; she is just trying to work things out and categorise them, as Evan himself might have done.

'No he's not,' says Stella.

Marjorie comes to the door with a pressure cooker full of pea soup. Linda is unable to quell a sudden, unexpected revulsion towards Marjorie. She hates the simpering, sympathetic look in Marjorie's eyes. But she says thank you and takes the soup and invites Marjorie in. The two women sit at the table. Linda is slowly lighting a cigarette, exaggeratedly nonchalant, as though nothing is amiss. Marjorie sits, blinking and nervous, trying to think of something to say. In the end she quotes from the Bible,

257

Matthew 5:4: *Blessed are those who mourn, for they will be comforted.* This is a mistake.

Linda starts raving on about all the problems that religion has brought to the world, how Marjorie is an uneducated person unable to think for herself and how she has no idea what is really going on and no imagination either.

Marjorie leaves by the front door, tears in her bulgy eyes. In the days afterwards, everyone is thankful for the house in between, the neutral territory next door. The two families avoid each other entirely.

Linda's deliberately wounding words ring in Marjorie's ears. Marjorie cries, on and off, for hours. And she thinks about the pressure cooker. She does not feel she can go back and get it; this useful piece of cookware is now lost forever.

Jo is on the moon. In the middle distance, there's an astronaut walking towards her. She realises it is her father, Evan Johnson. He is holding his goldfish-bowl headgear. He's delighted to see Jo, comes bounding towards her. She realises, with horror, that his face is nothing but a skull.

'What happened to your face?' asks Jo.

'It was eaten off by sharks,' says Evan matter-of-factly.

'Are you still alive?'

'No, 'fraid not.'

Jo screams, waking herself up with the raspy echo of a scream trying to break the surface of sleep. She lies there, remembering the sound of her father's voice.

Is it morning? Perhaps there's just the tiniest bit of light. Jo is desperately thirsty. She tries to roll out of bed but she is weighted down, entangled inside a grey army blanket. She struggles weakly, the blanket getting heavier. After a while, she decides to fall out of bed, blanket and all. She drags herself, trailing bedclothes, towards the window. Could that be a sliver of morning light coming in around the edges of the curtains? Maybe. Maybe not. Maybe it's just as dark as it was before.

In the strange transitional zone after Evan's death, Linda takes a job at the prawning factory, pulling the heads off prawns, getting spines caught in her fingernails. She rebuffs kindly overtures and invites those with a hint of danger. She discovers, and invites into her home, a different Port Badminton to the one she knew. She feels more comfortable with prawners and plantation workers who like to party hard. She hosts some big parties where people bring eels out of the river, crayfish, mangrove crabs, mangoes and bananas. They also bring large quantities of alcohol. She barely nods as she passes, in the street, the women who used to be her friends. She takes to wearing flowing cheesecloth, carrying out tie-dying experiments in the laundry. Linda's grip on where her children might be at any given time is now quite loose. Stella seems to be adapting, but for Jo everything is uncomfortable, unacceptable and wrong. This cannot possibly be her real life. Only the past, before The Fall, is real. She goes into suspended animation, hoping for order to be restored.

Linda does not make it up with Marjorie.

For a while Stella and Jo avoid the Kelly children. This is made easier by the fact that they are Condogs. But one day, before she has time to think about it, Stella finds herself playing with Susan on the footpath in front of the quiet house in the middle. And then she is playing down the side of the Kellys' house and then she is in the familiar back-yard itself. And then there are sleepovers at the Kellys', with three or four girls sharing a bathtub, giggling. Nothing is said about the galah. The cage is gone and there is a big heavy concrete planter there now, with a geranium in it. It's as if there never was a galah.

Eventually the Johnsons pack their things into the EH Holden and drive out of Clam Street. They drive out along the main road, blinkering to turn right at the T intersection. As they pass the Dish, it swivels slightly to watch them as they drive away.

THIRTEEN

Water

THERE IS A noise at the back door. For a fleeting moment I think it might be Lizzie coming home. She might be flapping in through the back door in her worn-down thongs, saying, 'Let's get the kettle on!'

But it's the grandniece. She comes towards me assertively. If I were a cat, I'd be hissing. If she tries to touch me I'll bite.

She looks at the mess of the *Lyrebird* and my droppings in disgust.

She changes direction and hunts about under the kitchen sink. She comes back armed with dustpan and brush.

'You're a messy beast,' she says. 'How did Aunty Lizzie put up with all this shit?'

She is speaking of Lizzie in the past tense.

'Stupid dickhead!' I shriek.

She goes out to the wheelie bin. I listen to the familiar sound of the lid whacking down. She reappears and heads for a drawer beside the kitchen sink. She roots around in it, turning around with a big pair of scissors in hand.

'Let's get you sorted out,' she says. As I struggle she holds me down on the table, cutting through the long flying feathers on one side. The pain goes searing through. She has cut into a blood feather!

I'm wounded, unbalanced. I sink my beak into her flesh, drawing blood.

We are fighting now, beak and claw. I'm fighting for my life, for what little I have.

She shakes me off and goes back to the kitchen sink. I lie gasping on the table, listening to the tap running. No doubt she is rinsing her wounds and applying bandaids. I feel the tears run over the bridge of my beak, dripping onto the table. What is to become of me?

Something dark flaps over me, a malevolent wraith. A bath towel. It's dark in here. I'm wrapped firmly, the way a baby is swaddled, or an insane person wrapped into a straightjacket, or six sausages rolled into newspaper at the butcher.

The wheel of fortune has turned. I'm being carried away from my home, from Lizzie, from hope. I am probably on the way to the vet to be euthanased. I can't tell, because, unlike Lizzie, this niece barely speaks to me.

Evan is getting lighter and lighter, rising vertically like Jesus. He rises up through the salt-spray air, into the cloudless blue sky. He rises through stratosphere, tropo-sphere, ionosphere and out into black space filled with glittering stars.

In the dark, in my towel, I can feel and hear the rhythm of walking.

'Incoming Kelly data,' says the Dish.

I don't reply. I'm on my death march.

'Lucky we had all those session handbags,' says Marj Kelly. 'I mean hessian sandbags.'

Marj is at the Civic Centre, staffing the Country Women's Association trestle table laden with sandwiches and an urn of boiling water. Sandbags and levee banks have saved the main township, but surrounding areas are under imminent threat of flooding in the aftermath of Steve.

Evacuees and homeless strays have been assembled here, accommodated on mattresses that line the large, echoing room. Marj is in her element, feeding them and giving them cups of tea and coffee. It reminds her of the evacuation in Geraldton, back when she was first married. Some of these same ladies – elderly now – were with her then.

Marjorie lifts the lid on the great CWA enamel teapot, the one that has seen duty through world wars, tropical festivals, cyclones, floods and one moon landing. She shovels in ten heaped teaspoons of leaves. Teabags would be easier, but Marj insists on loose leaves.

The evacuees rise up from their mattresses from time to time and come to the trestle table, mainly for something to do. They can have sandwiches now, but later they'll get hot meals on plastic plates under alfoil. There is a small blathering television set at the end of the hall. Clothes, pillows and toys spill from bags. An old brown dog, a set of guinea pigs in a cardboard box and three budgies in two cages are also present. Each of these has its own needs, to which the volunteers also apply themselves.

With Marjorie out, Kevin returns to his spot at the table, his writing pad open before him. A dozen eggs are boiling in a big pot on the stove. Kevin is under instructions to boil eggs for sandwiches for the evacuees. He will let them boil until the yolks go grey around the edges.

Kevin gets up from his letter and goes to stand just outside the back door. He farts freely and then decides, for inspiration, to listen to 'True Blue' by John Williamson. He goes to the living room and heads for the piece of furniture known as the Long Cupboard. Kevin opens the top drawer where audio tapes are kept. It is mostly a Greatest Hits collection, gifts over the years from the children. There are two compilations of Christmas songs, Roger Whittaker, Roger Miller, early Tom Jones. Kevin stands before the open drawer for a moment, letting the sight of the various tapes transport him to earlier times. There's Benny Hill with *Ernie (The Fastest Milkman in the West)*. But what he's looking for is the *True Blue* cassette tape, bought some years ago from the counter of the Caltex service station. It is the only musical purchase he has gone out and made for himself. His love of John Williamson came on later in life, after most of the family had gone. It represents a part of Kevin that the girls – remembering the characteristic Kevin of the 1960s and 70s – know nothing about. It doesn't occur to them that their father might be capable of evolving and changing, having a life of his own.

He walks back down the hall and into the kitchen, glancing at the jiggling eggs. The cassette player is on top of the fridge, coated in sticky dust. He puts the cassette in and presses play, but nothing happens except for the tiniest sense of a thwarted grinding. He ejects, turns it over, tries from the other side. It works. He leans back into the kitchen sink, listening, a delicious yearning welling in his chest.

True Blue, is it me and you?

Is it Mum and Dad? Is it a cockatoo?

Is it standin' by your mate when he's in a fight?

Or just Vegemite?

Pictures and sounds and smells come and go in Kevin's mind, some vague, some sharp. He thinks of men working, cigarettes hanging from their mouths, their hard, flat stomachs burned dark brown in the sun, cold Emu Bitter after a long hard shift, the sea at dawn, the sound of a prawning trawler, the wake behind. There's a flash of Mum poking at a mushrooming sheet in a wood-fired copper in the backyard, and Dad in a khaki uniform, the thick prickly feel of it, like a blanket. And the cockatoo . . . he remembers that he used to have a cockatoo. A pink and grey one. Kevin glances down at a big concrete planter standing beside the back door, a geranium growing lushly in it, the deep green of the leaves, the velvety scarlet of the flowers. *Where is my cockatoo?* For some reason the thought of the lost pink and grey galah sends the tears welling up over the bottom lids of Kevin's eyes. There are galahs everywhere, of course. Flying overhead, sitting on powerlines, crowding into treetops. There are galahs for the taking. But what about *that* galah?

That particular galah is never coming back, and nor are Mum or Dad or hard brown stomachs or cigarettes. Kevin is frankly wallowing now, as Williamson continues to aim arrows into his heart.

The song ends. Kevin pulls his weight away from the sink, takes one step across the width of the small kitchen, and presses the stop button. In the silence, he stands with his arms over the top of the fridge, cradling the cassette player.

Or just Vegemite?

Kevin's hand reaches for the plastic bag of sliced white bread, baked locally under the banner of the nationwide Tip Top franchise. He fiddles with the tiny square of hard plastic that the soft thin bag is gathered into, releases it, shakes out four floppy slices. Margarine out of the fridge, the slightly warm Vegemite jar out of the cupboard. He makes himself sandwiches, spreading first the margarine thickly, then the friendly dark substance thinly. He cuts across and across again, creating little squares, not triangles like the ones Marj makes to serve at functions and fund-raisers. Kevin enjoys being alone in Marj's kitchen, doing what he likes. He gets a bit of margarine into the Vegemite jar and leaves it in there, carelessly.

He takes his plate of sandwiches back to the dining room table, back to the homework he has set himself.

I never made any headway, he writes to Kimberly Lamb.

He realises he can be completely honest with her.

He sits at the table and thinks about making headway, about early dreams of making enough money to be comfortable. He had never aspired to rich, just comfortable. But what exactly does he mean by comfortable? Does he want to move out of this house into a two-storey brick house?

He thinks about Susan in her palace on the outskirts of Perth. Three bathrooms, including a bathroom just for the kids. All that cleaning.

No, that's not what he wants. This laminex table, this backyard, this toilet: they are his life. He eases himself down on the familiar black plastic toilet seat, no longer new. Does he want to travel? Not particularly. Overseas, Over East . . . the imagined difficulties involved – hassles at airports – seem to outweigh the benefits. By comfortable, he simply means not having to worry about money. Not to have to think about whether the can of peas is ninety-two cents or one dollar twenty. To buy each of the girls something nice, like a bracelet or a necklace from the jeweller's. Or a locket. He realises this is an old desire of his, no longer relevant. The girls wouldn't want a locket. He doesn't know what they would want.

To eat steak more often, rissoles less often. That would be nice. He washes his hands after the toilet, sits down again at the kitchen table and thinks of words he might write:

I always wanted my own boat. I always wanted to stand at the wheel of my own boat, to look up at the rigging, the nets, to count them all as mine. I wanted to look at the catch and consider it all my own. This boat, I wanted to hand down to my son.

Kevin's mind drifts resentfully to Thomas 'Crowbar' Wilson, the man who made headway all his life. Who always had the wind behind him.

*

269

When Marj gets back from the Civic Centre, she finds Kevin standing in the dining room, not going forward or backwards, just standing. He has the look of a dog who meets you at the front door but guiltily, because it is thinking about all the washing it has brought down off the clothesline out the back. Marjorie's body is tired but her eyes dart about a bit, from habit. Nothing seems particularly amiss, other than Kevin himself.

Kevin: 'How's it going down the poor?'

Marj: 'All right, Kev. A couple of backpackers tried to get themselves a free hot meal.'

Kevin: 'Bloody freeloaders! Did you give 'em whatfor?'

Marj: 'And I've had a rotten headache all day.'

Kevin: 'Why don't you have a cup of tea and a –'

Marj: 'No more tea for me, Kev, I'm awash.'

Kevin nods and sits down at the table, in front of his cold half-cup of instant coffee and the crossword page of the *West Australian*. He picks up the pen, casually, and does a little scribble on the white margin, as if testing to see if the pen will go.

Marj goes out to the toilet, and then comes back through the dining room, glancing over Kevin's shoulder as she goes past, taking in the empty crossword puzzle and the squiggle. She fiddles around at the sink and dries her hands on a tea towel. The bowl of warm boiled eggs on the bench is like a tribute, like a vase of roses.

'Thanks, Kev,' she says. She comes and stands behind his chair and gives him an awkward hug across the shoulders. As she does so, she allows herself to go a little bit weak, leaning into him, taking some comfort and energy from him.

'Can you peel the eggs for me, Kev? Keep the shells for the compost.'

'No worries, love.'

'I'm just going to finish the little what's-it.'

'Righto.'

Marj settles back at her sewing machine, threads the needle, checks the bobbin. Sewing is a familiar, soothing activity. But this project is small and fiddly. It takes all her concentration.

It is an order from Gemma, the Aboriginal girl who works out on the islands, looking after small native what's-its-names. Bandicoots?

'Bloody galah bites and shits everywhere,' Gemma had said. 'Can you make me some of these little nappies?'

And she'd shown a page out of a bird magazine, titled 'Flight Suits'.

'Sorry about Old Lizzie,' Marj had said.

'She had a good innings.'

There will be a big funeral, with people coming from all directions. After that, Gemma's family will be moving into the house in Oyster Street.

Carefully shaped, the bird nappy has elastic straps that fit over the wings, a velcro closure over the back, an opening for the tail and a pouch for droppings. This pouch is designed to take cut-down ladies' panty liners, to 'protect the suit and keep the bird comfortable'. A small loop over the velcro closure can be used to attach a lanyard to 'prevent dangerous fly-aways'.

Marj is not sure what she should charge for this unusual little job. She has used scraps of fabric from her own collection, so there's only labour to charge for. Gemma has a government job, a nice car. She decides to charge quite a lot.

She snips the thread. That's done. Prototype complete.

Marj feels tired and heavy. She gets up from her sewing chair and wanders into the bedroom for a nap. She unbuckles her sandals and puts them neatly together on the floor on her side of the bed. She takes off her glasses and places them on the tea chest. She shakes out a slip of folded paper from a small yellow box of Bex powders that lives there on the chest, and lifts a fine crocheted cover off the top of a tall glass of water. The tiny blue glass beads clink against the glass. She pours the powder onto her tongue and follows up with a deep swig, and then another. She fluffs up her pillow, arranges her sheet, and passes immediately into deep sleep.

Marjorie dreams she is standing on the main street, watching the floats of the Tropical Festival Parade go past. At first, it seems there is nothing out of the ordinary, although the colours are strangely vivid, like in those old Technicolour films. Somehow, she is simultaneously at her place on the footpath but also floating above the parade, able to see it as a whole. She sees the camels with teenagers feigning boredom on their backs, and the hospital float with its mad cross-eyed surgeon and lashings of blood. There is a bedraggled brass band unable to quite reach its notes, all as usual; there are astronauts in full regalia on the back of a flatbed truck, in the company of Aboriginal men and women in chains, manacled together.

Marjorie catches sight of Linda Johnson and Harry Baumgarten in the parade, walking side by side in silver sandals, leading a bevy of marching Brownies. Linda is wearing a silver minidress; Harry is wearing only his briefest swimming trunks. He has a remarkably good body. Now Marjorie wants to stay in the dream, to get a good look at Linda's dress. Who made it? But someone is knocking at the door. As she wakes she tries to hold that last image but it vanishes; she is aware she has been dreaming but the images have all drained away.

Marjorie remains still on the bed, her eyes open, the rest of her body immobile. It is as if she has just come to the surface from the bottom of the ocean. Eventually, she swings her legs over the side of the bed and shuffles her feet into her unbuckled sandals and slaps out to the front door.

We are standing at Marj's front door, listening to the quiet scuffle of someone on the other side. I'm still bundled in my towel, but I've been given a hole to peer out of.

Marj appears, blinking like someone who has just woken up. Her face is older but unmistakeable. Her eyes still have that automatic kindness when they look at people; she still glances at me as if I were a *thing*.

'Hi, Marj! We're here for the fitting,' says Gemma. She holds up the bundle of me, to indicate who is to have the fitting.

I notice how Gemma has said 'we'. A little *couply*, if you ask me.

'Hello, cocky!' says Marj perfunctorily. She'll never be a bird person.

As we pass into the interior of the house, I'm aware of the familiar, forgotten smell of the Kelly household. As we pass from hall into kitchen, the bead curtain drapes itself through hair and feather, needs to be shrugged off.

'I'll just pop the kettle on,' says Marj. A flash of light glints off the stainless-steel kettle as she lifts it into the sink to fill. She opens a new packet of ginger nut biscuits.

I'm desperate for a biscuit.

Gemma takes a seat and lets me hop down onto the table. I waddle over to inspect the writing pad that is sitting there, pages folded back, revealing four or five lines written in shaky blue ballpoint.

Your a very attractive woman. We could go out dancing.

Through the screen door, I can make out the toilet in the backyard. The door is shut. I can sense Kevin Kelly in there, taking his time, just like the old days.

'Lucky likes to have a cup of tea,' says Gemma. 'Keep it weak, though.'

'Righto,' says Marj, and gets out another cup.

'A bit of tea is all right for a galah – it's got tannins in it, just like the tannins in water that galahs drink in the wild,' says Gemma. Unlike Lizzie, she talks freely in company.

'Ke-ev!' calls Marj. 'Cuppa tea!'

There is silence from the backyard.

'How are your bandicoots and whatnot?' asks Marj, as she

puts four mugs on the table and the sugar bowl, a jug of milk, and spoons and the plate of biscuits.

Leaving the tea to draw, Marj nips out to get my suit. I want a biscuit so badly I could explode. But I wait.

When she reappears, holding the little article of clothing out towards me, I recognise the fabric. It is the same as Linda Johnson's Moon Ball dress.

That long-ago moment comes back to me: Linda Johnson twirling in the backyard, her hair falling out of its bobby pins, the little girls clapping.

The gown was never worn, never paid for. Events over-took it.

Marj and Gemma's hands are all over me, pulling things this way and that. 'It'll need a dart here,' says Marj, just as she used to say to the ladies who came for their fittings. Then they stand back to look. There's a diamante button on the front, at the breastbone.

I have a place at the table. A cup of tea. A biscuit. A Moon Ball gown. I could swoon. I let out a happy double chirrup.

'She likes it!' says Gemma.

I twirl on the table top, imagining my hair swinging.

Marjorie catches sight of Kevin's handwriting on the open writing pad. Her bulgy eyes lock on, flaring with curi-osity. She's trying to read the upside-down writing as she half listens to Gemma talking about the Shark Bay mouse.

The toilet flushes, the screen door swings and there is a masculine clearing of the throat. Marjorie's hand has stretched out to turn the writing pad around, to have a good look, but now Kevin Kelly has joined us, with his red face, thin grey hair and large belly with a blue shirt stretched over it. His own hand reaches the writing pad before Marjorie's. He whips it away and hugs it to his chest.

'Who've you been writing to, Kev?' asks Marjorie.

Kevin looks at Gemma, his mouth open and working slightly, trying to think of something.

Kevin glances at me in my ball gown and looks again. It's a *double take*.

'Is that our cocky?' says Kevin, pointing at me. 'The one we lost?'

'Don't be silly, Kev!' says Marj. But she looks at me, really looking into my eyes this time.

Everyone goes silent. They gaze at me in my Moon Ball gown, holding my bit of biscuit in one claw, nibbling steadily. There is silence. It is a long, beautiful silence; the silence of surrendering all ideas about anything.

Kevin picks up the newspaper, subtly folding the writing pad into it. He walks over to the stove and takes the box of matches from a knobbly glazed ceramic pot and hurries back out through the flyscreen. He disappears behind the toilet.

*

Kevin is standing before the blackened forty-four-gallon drum that serves as family incinerator. With the back of his hand, he nudges at the sheet of rusted metal that acts as a lid, letting it drop on the ground. Kevin stands there, the newspaper and writing pad in one hand, matches in the other. Did Marjorie see what he'd written? He cannot bear to read back over his own words, but they repeat themselves nauseatingly in his head. *Your a very attractive woman. We could go out dancing.* He tears pages out of the writing pad, scrunching them into burnable balls. He takes great hanks of newsprint and scrunches those as well. He lights the paper, watches the orange flames lick up tall. The bikini girl and her palm trees succumb to the flames.

Gemma and I are heading back down Clam Street. Branches are down; the street is littered with post-cyclone debris.

'I don't actually believe in birds as pets,' she says. 'You fullas should be flying free. But you'd be useless out on your own, wouldn't you?'

She tries to put me on her shoulder, to carry me the way Lizzie did. Her handling is all wrong. Her shoulder is plumper than Lizzie's. I have to dig my claws in a little tighter to get a grip.

'Don't you dare bite me again!' she says.

Her ear is so close, so tempting. With difficulty, I resist.

We look out over the samphire flat. A couple of seagulls are flying in the distance. I would indeed be useless out on my own.

I settle myself on Gemma's shoulder, tuning myself to the rhythm of her gait. I make a mental note to work on my jealousy issues.

The floodwaters have risen over the banks of the Sandhurst River. Great chunks of the banks have been washed away. Silt is coming down from miles inland. The brown river sends watery feelers out across the land, finding whole boxes of fruit and vegetables and the odd wooden chair. It curls itself around these things, bringing them into the main current, pushing them out to the open ocean.

Underneath the Dish, the grizzled old Dogger presses the rewind button on his VHS tape. He has been on a movie-watching binge. He hasn't been out shooting for years, but he has been lucky: he has been given the job of temporary caretaker here at the Dish until work begins on making it a proper tourist attraction, complete with interpretive signage. It's somewhere to live, and pays well enough to cover drinks and meals at the Port Hotel. During the cyclone, with the wind howling and rattling outside, he was quite snug, indulging himself in memories of Linda Johnson.

His reverie is interrupted by the arrival of the men who will take the Dish out of lock and put it back in its usual position looking down over the residents of Port Badminton.

I hear a blast of static, a Dishly clearing of the throat.

DISH: I've got the answer.
GALAH: What was the question?
DISH: Didn't you want to know about Evan Johnson? Did he jump or did he fall?
GALAH: Oh yes. What was he thinking?
DISH: Midway down, the falling man pauses to open his arms and embrace the entire Indian Ocean. Silver fish leap out of the water and glint in the sunlight. He feels

cool water running down his chest. He holds his hand
up to the water breaking through the skin of his neck.
He presses down on the pulsing vein, feeling the liquid
seeping through his fingers. He cups his hand, fills it with
water, and takes it to his mouth. It tastes cool and fresh
and pure. He gorges on the water and then stops, satisfied,
letting it run down his legs, off his toes.

He looks down at the water smashing and roiling on the
rocks below and thinks:

$$F = \frac{GM_1M_2}{r^2}$$

GALAH: Roger that.

A Note on the Dish

THE READER MIGHT be interested to know that in the north-west of Western Australia, there is a red dune just outside the town of Carnarvon. A large white dish sits there, overlooking the town. This is a decommissioned Overseas Telecommunications Commission dish and it did not play a role in tracking the 1969 Apollo mission. However, a little way along the dune, there are concrete footings and traces of another dish – an FPQ radar, long dismantled – that *did* track that giant leap.

Acknowledgements

I WOULD LIKE to thank: Peter Bishop for always knowing what this novel was, even before I did; Leah Kaminsky for championing it; Charlotte Wood for top-shelf writerly advice; Jacinta di Mase for agreeing to represent it; Geordie Williamson and Mathilda Imlah at Picador for publishing it; Bruce Fell for a wonderful conversation about the capabilities of the Dish; the Australia Council for a $5000 Emerging Writers Grant in 2005; Varuna the Writers' House; Penguin for a $5000 editing scholarship in 2010; Merrill Findlay, who wrote a book about my home town; Tony Savdié for help with an airfare; my friends Anna Feord, Vince Melton, Steph Luke, Angela Matheson, Ian Pitt, Martha Gelin, Jane Roffe, Karen Golland, Dawn Nusa, Adrian Symes, Lisa Bostock, Helen Bergen, Ray Mjadwesch and Ali Foley (and others), who read the slow-forming manuscript and encouraged me to continue; Jim and Alison Gregg, Hamish Lindsay and Steve Keogh for sharing their stories of the space race in a small town (all technical absurdities mine); and my partner Steve Woodhall for calmly keeping me afloat every time I thought my ship was sinking. I also wish to thank the red earth, the glittering sea and the underground river that kept me company through my childhood and all the people, animals, plants, insects and other things I found in that particular place on earth, including the moon and the night sky. And I thank my sister Deb Sorensen and parents Brian and Yvonne Sorensen for being with me always.